Reflections in the water

Rachele Modiano Mendes - The Early Years
Book 1

Silvano Stagni

Perpetuum Mobile Publishing

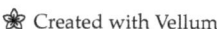

To Elena, who followed in her great-grandmother's footsteps and Louisa who has inherited her great-grandmother's no-nonsense approach.

Also by Silvano Stagni

Villa Kalman's Secrets

Venice 1925. Somebody shoots at two teenagers who jumped a fence to retrieve a ball from Villa Kalman's garden. A couple of months later, a young man is found severely beaten and unconscious in the shed of the same villa. Who fired the shot? Who was the young man? Why was he beaten unconscious? Were those events related? Rachele Modiano Mendes is pregnant with her second child. She needs to unravel Villa Kalman's secrets before she starts a leave of absence from work.

Book 2 of Rachele Modiano Mendes - The Early Years

(Preview at the end)

The Dressmaker's Parcels

The story of the Modiano Mendes clan during Mussolini's racial laws, World War II, and the Holocaust. Spoiler: Rachele and her eldest daughter Emma join the resistance.

Available on Amazon

Elena's Memory

Venice, 1947. The search for the legitimate heir to a couple who did not survive the camps brings a young woman who lost her memory to Venice. The love and support of the extended Modiano-Mendes clan helps her recover her memory. They soon realise that the attempts to get rid of her had nothing to do with the inheritance.

The first book of the series: Rachele Modiano Mendes investigates

Available on Amazon

Unconditional

A collection of feel-good short stories about acceptance, love, and memories.

Available on Amazon

Foreword

Before we discuss the characters of this book, a note on the names used by Italian married women. In Italy, a woman does not change her maiden name. She has three legal names:

- **Her maiden name**. For instance, Rachele's law qualifications predate her marriage, so she uses her maiden name professionally, so she is Avvocato Modiano (In Italy, professionals have titles according to their profession. Avvocato is the Italian for lawyer.)
- **Her maiden name and her husband's name.** For instance, Rachele is referred to as Rachele Modiano Mendes because she is married to Gabriele Mendes.
- **Her husband's name.** Rachele would be Mrs Mendes, or Rachele Mendes.

A married woman can choose among three legal signatures. She could sign using any of the three variations listed above.

Another example is the countess. She was born Deborah Camerini, and married Count Pesaro De Bonfili. So her choice of three signatures would have been (when Italy was a Kingdom):

- Deborah Camerini
- Deborah Camerini, Countess Pesaro de Bonfili
- Countess Pesaro de Bonfili

All the children of her friend, Fiamma Andrade Mendes, and their spouses, also known as 'Aunt Deborah'.

The Mendes family from Venice

Samuele Mendes (born 1870), **Fiamma Andrade** (born 1873) – married in 1894

- **Raffaele Mendes** (born 1895), married to **Antonella Levi**
- **Gabriele Mendes** (born 1897), married to **Rachele Modiano**
- **Emanuele Mendes** (born 1902)
- **Myriam Mendes** (born 1905),
- **Roberto Mendes** (born 1913)

The Modiano family from Trieste

Baron Davide Modiano (born 1860) married to **Esther Coronel** (born 1866)

- **Greta Modiano** (b. 1885), married to **Michele Treves** **– they have not made alyah yet.**
- (Children not mentioned in the book)
- **Michele Modiano** (born 1887), married to **Stella Basevi**
- **Maximilian Modiano** (b. 1912), **Paola Modiano** (b.1915), **Alex Modiano** (b. 1919)
- **Sarah Modiano** (born 1888), married to **Hans Basevi**
- (Children not mentioned in the book)
- **Celeste Modiano** (born 1890), married to **Maximilian Attard**

- (Children not mentioned in the book)
- **Daniele Modiano** (born 1891), engaged to **Perla Oppenheim**
- **Ricardo Modiano** (born 1894), married to **Hannah Sarah Cohen**
- (Children not mentioned in the book)
- **Rachele Modiano** (born 1898), married to **Gabriele Mendes**
- **Barbara Modiano (born 1900), not yet married to Herbert Cohen**

The Pesaro de Bonfili family from Venice

Count Victor Pesaro De Bonfili (born 1865), **Deborah Camerini** (born 1873) – married in 1898

- **Giorgio Pesaro De Bonfili** (born 1902)
- **Sarah Pesaro De Bonfili** (born 1905)

Other characters

Franco Venier – Lead partner of the Venier-Zanin law firm, he becomes Rachele's boss

Giovanni Zanin – the other partner in the Venier-Zanin law firm

Alvise Cantoni – A childhood friend of Gabriele Mendes, also a lawyer (born 1897)

Paolo Mondani – A childhood friend of Gabriele Mendes (born 1897), married to **Sofia Taiman Mondani** (born 1897)

- **Arrigo Mondani** – Paolo and Sofia's son (born in 1918)

Adalberto Medici – an art expert

Carlo Simoni – an art dealer

Franco Pavan – the owner of an alleged Turner

Isabella Pavan Rossi – Mario's married daughter

Stefano Baldan – An accountant and a professional executor of wills

Antonio Penzo – a magistrate at the Venice court

Danilo Saradei – The heir of Count Federico Maichich, an aristocrat with a quirky hobby

Gino Rigoni – An enforcer

Chapter One

Gabriele Mendes and Rachele Modiano had been married for only three months. They had met eighteen months earlier when friends of their families, the Count and Countess Pesaro De Bonfili, invited them to a Friday night dinner. They looked into each other's eyes and they felt a strong chemistry.

Gabriele's mother and Deborah Camerini, Countess Pesaro De Bonfili, had been close friends since they met in primary school. He knew his honorary aunt Deborah had other plans. She hoped that Rachele would end up marrying her son, Giorgio and Gabriele was invited to assess his interest for one of her eldest brother's daughters. He was embarrassed he had disrupted them. However, Deborah Camerini's plans were at such an early stage that she passed on to her next choice for a potential daughter-in-law with no bad feelings for her honorary nephew.

Countess Pesaro De Bonfili and her husband were supposed to leave for their summer holidays right after the young couple's wedding. She had told them she would invite them to tea to give them her wedding present after everybody had come back to Venice. She abandoned her original idea for a wedding present after she had Gabriele's parents for dinner. Her new idea for a present was much more appropriate, but it would not have been ready before the wedding.

Gabriele was very familiar with the Pesaro De Bonfili residence. He had been there many times and had fond memories of the smaller sitting room with its blue upholstery. In his childhood, he used to play by the window. It was only Rachele's second visit, and she was nervous. Her parents were close friends of the Count and Countess, but she had never accompanied her parents when they travelled to Venice to visit them.

They were now in the larger sitting room, the one with red wallpaper and large windows overlooking the Grand Canal. Tonia, the housekeeper, had told them the Countess apologised and would join them in a few minutes. Rachele found the room intimidating, but it was also the place where she and Gabriele had seen each other for the first time. She felt mellow and uneasy. They were sitting on a small two-seater couch facing the windows. They enjoyed their closeness. Silence between them was never uncomfortable.

When they heard the door open, they stood up and turned around. Gabriele showed familiarity with somebody he had known all his life; he smiled at the countess, called her Aunt Deborah, kissed her hand, and hugged her. Rachele was more formal in her greetings. Deborah Camerini sensed she had to show she was ready to welcome Rachele into her world and gave her a kiss on both cheeks.

"You look so glamorous together. The first time you come as a married couple. I claim the credit for this marriage."

The Countess sat on the arm-chair closer to Rachele, her face trying to convey a warm welcome for her new honorary niece.

"Rachele, I love your dress. Wearing green makes your amazing eyes stand out. Thank you for coming to collect your present. A porter will deliver it to home tomorrow morning. It is too big for you to carry it home."

Countess Pesaro Bonfili got up and went for the bell. A plump woman appeared carrying a painting in a way that made it impossible for Gabriele and Rachele to see what it was. She carefully put it down behind the sofa where Gabriele and Rachele were sitting.

"Thank you, Rosa, you can serve coffee in about ten minutes". The Countess picked up the painting and started turning it slowly.

"A week before your wedding, I had Fiamma and Samuele for dinner. They told me where they had bought a home for you, and I realised I had your perfect wedding. It is a painting by a pupil of Canaletto. It used to be in my bedroom when I was a child, it shows the campo[1] where you live. Look here on the left, that is the palazzo where your home is."

Gabriele and Rachele looked at the painting. It showed their new home. One room was visible through the large open window. You could see the top of an armchair, where their sitting room was. They thanked the countess. Rachele was still being formal. Rosa came back with a trolley with coffee, cups and saucers, and some cakes. The Countess stood up.

"Thank you, Rosa. Rachele, please, call me Aunt Deborah. Everybody in the Mendes family does, except Fiamma and Samuele, of course. You are now part of the Mendes family, therefore I am your honorary aunt. Leave this countess business to strangers!"

Rachele was still not ready for familiarity, but she knew she had better comply.

"Thank you, countess... I mean, thank you, Aunt Deborah."

The Countess smiled while she was cutting the cake.

"See, it is easy. By the way, I understand your father is coming to Venice tomorrow. He and my husband have a meeting at a law firm in Rialto. You should ask him to introduce you if you want to practise law."

Rachele was surprised that the countess mentioned work in a matter-of-fact way. There were few women with a law degree, there were even fewer who practised law after they got married.

"I had already thought of that. My parents arrive tomorrow morning. I think the meeting at the law firm is after lunch. I plan to discuss it with my father over lunch. My mother will support me.."

"I am sure she will, and convincing your father will not require a lot of effort. What do you think, Gabriele?"

Gabriele was lost in his thoughts. He liked his honorary aunt. He knew he married a strong woman and was watching the interaction between those two important women in his life, hoping to notice the beginning of a friendship, or at least non-belligerence.

"What do I think about what, Aunt Deborah?"

"Rachele working, Baron Modiano introducing his daughter to a law firm, etc."

Gabriele realised he had to be very careful. The potential for irritating either of the two women was very high. He also wondered what prompted his aunt to ask his opinion.

"Well, I knew Rachele would want to work. I do not mind, it is her choice. After all, you and my mother work."

"Your mother started working when your sister Myriam was old enough to go to school and she works with your father in the family business. I buy art on behalf of clients. Most of

4

them are friends of ours who do not live in Venice. Our days are flexible and we can also be there for our husbands. Rachele will have to go to an office every day."

"I do not see the difference. Rachele can be there for me and I can be there for her. We plan to hire a housekeeper. Do you know how we can go about finding one?"

"I'll ask around. However, you both have to be prepared for a lot of questions, even unpleasant comments about Rachele working."

Gabriele felt the need to hold his wife's hand. Somehow, he both needed and offered support.

"I do not care. I found the job I always wanted and will stop being the bookkeeper for the family business. I am sure my parents told you I will start working for the city of Venice next month, in the office that manages the canals and the upkeep of the facades of buildings that face a canal."

The conversation continued until the Countess excused herself. She had to write to two clients to update them on what she had found for them in an art gallery near Rialto and in an antique shop in Murano. Gabriele and Rachele thanked her for the coffee and for the beautiful wedding present and left.

They walked towards the waterbus stop. The vaporetto was the only form of public transport in Venice. Rachele was still new to the city, and she had not yet developed the internal map that allows Venetians to walk around without getting lost. Gabriele led the way.

When they were on the vaporetto, Rachele started discuss the painting.

"It was very generous of Aunt Deborah to give us a painting that was in her bedroom when she was a child, she must have been very fond of it"

Gabriele checked that there were nobody he knew witing earshot.

"Undoubtedly she wanted to give us something she loved. It was very sweet of her"

"You sound very matter of fact, don't you like it?"

"I would not have bought it. I love it, we'll hang it in the living room above the sofa, but it will be a cherished possession, but I hope we shall buy better artwork over time."

Rachele whispered back.

"I wouldn't have bought it either but I think it shows how much Countes…I mean Aunt Deborah is fond of you and has accepted me."

The vaporetto stopped at San Stae. They got off, and Rachele asked Gabriele to let her find a way home, to Campo San Giacomo Dall'Orio, to see if she remembered the way. She had to learn.

A porter appeared with the painting all wrapped up early the following morning. Gabriele had taken the day off from running the administration for the Mendes silk company. They unwrapped the painting and hung it in the sitting room. They sat on the sofa, looking at it. The world outside was just a haze when they were together. Soon the doorbell brought them back down to earth. Baron Modiano and his wife, Rachele's parents, had arrived from Trieste. Gabriele stood up to open the door. Rachele went to talk to the maid to see which refreshments were available for her parents.

It was not the first time that Baron Davide Modiano and his wife, Esther Coronel Modiano, had visited their home. Gabriele was beginning to feel at ease around them, at least when they were in his own territory. His parents-in-law had a very matter-of-fact and pragmatic attitude towards life. Once they accepted him, they treated him as one of the family, no excessive formality, no pretensions, just good manners and pragmatism. Rachele appeared after Gabriele had taken her parents' coats and hats.

"We have organised refreshments in the sitting room. A light lunch will be ready in about an hour. Gabriele's parents invited us to dinner tonight. I thought we did not need a big lunch."

They moved to the sitting room. Rachele was serving coffee and the cake she had baked earlier when her mother noticed the painting.

"That painting was not here when we came a month ago. Did you commission it?"

Rachele handed her the plate with a slice of a pistachio cake.

"That is Aunt Deborah's wedding present. Countess Pesaro de Bonfili gave it to us yesterday. A porter delivered it this morning."

"Why do you call her Aunt Deborah?"

"Aunt Deborah and Fiamma have been close friends since childhood. Gabriele and his siblings call her aunt, and her children call Fiamma aunt. The countess told me to call her aunt since I am now part of the Mendes family."

Baron Modiano had finished eating the cake, put down the plate, and took a sip of coffee.

"It is nice of her and Fiamma. We have close friends, but I never thought of suggesting that you and your siblings call them uncle or aunt. You have too many uncles and aunts without adding any honorary one. By the way, this cake is excellent."

Gabriele was proud of his wife, whatever she was doing, but he loved her baking skills.

"Baron Modiano, I am very grateful that you decided your children had to have a trade up their sleeves, just in case. I am happy Rachele chose to become a master baker while she was studying law."

Esther smiled. It had been her idea.

Baron Modiano and Count Pesaro De Bonfili had spent the previous two hours going through the details of a joint investment with Franco Venier, the senior partner in the Venier-Zanin law firm. Baron Modiano sounded well-prepared. His comments had impressed the lawyer. As Franco Venier was walking his clients to the door, he had to find out why.

"Baron Modiano, please apologise to my being curious. Did you study law? In the last two hours, you made the right comments at the right time and you understood some delicate legal issues."

Davide Modiano was proud of his children and had no problem showing it.

"No, I did not. My daughter Rachele did. She was the only woman to study law in her year at the University and worked for a year with my solicitor in Trieste before getting married and moving to Venice. She went through the paperwork this morning."

"She briefed you very well."

"Rachele is looking for a job. Would you talk to her?"

"Again, based on how well she briefed you, I would like to meet her."

Gabriele was used to waking up before his wife. That morning, he woke up to find Rachele getting dressed.. She was sorting out her skirt and had noticed her husband stirring.

"Did I wake you up?"

Gabriele looked at the alarm clock on his bedside.

"No, this is the time I wake up in the morning. Are you nervous?"

"Yes, I am not cut out to be a decoration on my husband's arm. I need to work. If this morning goes well, I might have a job by this afternoon."

Gabriele picked up his dressing gown from the armchair.

"You will have a job by this afternoon."

"Do you mind?"

"It is your choice. I hope we live our lives together in a way that allows us to pursue our own goals. I'll be by your side, whatever you do, and I hope you will always be by mine."

Rachele turned around and hugged him. Gabriele kissed his wife.

Rachele had her meeting with Franco Venier at 10.30. She walked with Gabriele to his in-law's warehouse, which was next to their home in the last extension of the Ghetto and spent some time talking to Fiamma, discussing plans for the forthcoming Jewish High Holidays. Her young sister-in-law, Myriam, was spending the day at the beach with friends and offered to walk with her to Rialto. She could take the waterbus to the Lido near the bridge. Rachele welcomed the company. She hated to admit how nervous she was, even to herself. She was glad to have company, and she was also relieved that she did not have to worry about getting lost. They arrived outside the law firm too early. Rachele decided to walk with her to the waterbus stop. She had just started calling it *vaporetto* like a local. She walked back looking at shop windows to kill time and rang the doorbell or the Venier-Zanin law firm precisely at 10.30. Her nerves kicked in as she was climbing the stairs to the first floor. She had never had a job interview before. Her previous job as a trainee lawyer was at the law firm that handled all the legal needs of her family business. The account was large enough to get her a job as a trainee lawyer. This time, she felt she was on her own.

The office was in Calle Dell'Aquila Nera[2]. She wondered whether it was a message. The black eagle was a symbol of the Habsburg dynasty. She took it as a good omen; she was born when Trieste was still part of the Austrian empire. When she walked into the office, a secretary took her to a small meeting room with a big window where she could see a bit of Rialto bridge. She stood by the window, lost in her thoughts until she heard someone coughing behind her.

"Good morning, I am Franco Venier. I assume you are Rachele Modiano."

"Rachele Modiano Mendes."

"Of course you are married. Marriage brought you to Venice, and now you would like to make use of your law degree. What does your husband think?"

"My husband thinks it is up to me. He supports whatever I decide to do."

"Great. First, let me congratulate for the way you briefed your father. He asked well thought out questions, and somebody had obviously already gone through the paperwork, discussed its main points with him, and told him how feasible each request for change would have been."

"Since I graduated, my father always shows me any legal paperwork he has to sign. I hope you do not mind. I am used to keeping what I read for myself."

"It is unusual for a woman to practice law. It is even more unusual for the married daughter of an aristocrat to practice law. What can you tell me to reassure me you will not stop working when you and your husband decide to have a baby?"

"There is very little I can say. My eldest sister, Greta, is a surgeon, married to another doctor. They have three children, and she is expecting the fourth. Another sister, Sarah, works in a bank in Trieste. She is also married with two children. Another sister, Celeste, works in the family company. She is engaged. My younger sister Barbara is studying biology at the University of Trieste."

"An impressive family, are you likely to follow in your sisters' path?"

"Yes, I know you may consider me a bet, but I am a bet you will win. I graduated with top marks. I had to be the best to survive as the only woman in my class. I love finding the implications of any sentence of a contract I read. I am sure you will not regret the decision to bet on me."

"I have not decided to hire you, at least not yet."

Rachele's nerves were taking over, but she kept a calm outward appearance. She smiled and added.

"I hope you will. I think I will love working with you."

Franco Venier looked at his watch, told Rachele he had to prepare for another meeting but will be in touch with his decision by the end of the following day. He had to consult his partner.

Chapter Two

October 1921

Beginning a new job during the month of the Jewish High holidays was a challenge, most Jews would not work the two days of the Jewish New Year (Rosh Hashanah) and the day and a half of the Day of Atonement (Yom Kippur), traditional Jews would take four more days off for the holiday of Succoth. Luckily, Rachele's boss had Jewish friends, so she had very little explaining to do. Gabriele insisted he walked with her to work every morning. It was a way to spend more time together before their respective day caught up with them. Rachele was still under the magic spell of the Most Serene City, *La Serenissima*, as it called itself when it was at the top of its power. Every morning they stopped for a short while at the top of Rialto Bridge to look at the Grand Canal. Rachele called it 'her *Canaletto* moment'. When they reached the entrance to the building where Rachele's office was, Gabriele kissed his wife on the cheek and walked to his office.

Rachele was a trainee. She did not see clients without a partner or a more senior colleague. That morning, Count Pesaro De Bonfili asked to see her for a personal matter. He would not take more than half an hour of her time. Rachele's puzzled expression when she entered the meeting room made the count smile. A secretary came in with coffee for the visitor; after she left, the count came straight to the point.

"I have a minor problem I would like to keep in the family as much as possible. You are the daughter of an old friend of mine and the wife of one of Deborah's honorary nephews. You are family."

Rachele felt the need to say something

"I hope it is something that does not require a lot of experience."

The count smiled, took a sip of the water the receptionist had brought with the coffee, and continued.

"I hope not. I think it takes a bright legal mind and somebody who cares enough for my wife to protect her from any legal problems."

Rachele stood up to fetch a notepad and a pencil that were on a side table. She wanted to be ready to take notes and give time to the count to organise his thoughts.

"As you know, my wife helps people sell art or finds art for eager buyers. Almost all her clients are friends and acquaintances. They trust her. There is more than trust at stake if something goes wrong. The good name of our family must be protected."

"I thought she uses her maiden name, Deborah Camerini."

"Yes, she does. However, most of her clients know she is Countess Pesaro de Bonfili. Anyway, whatever name she uses needs to be protected. A business acquaintance of mine asked her to help a friend of his sell a painting. The friend, Franco Pavan, invited us to his house near Dolo last Sunday and we saw it. I recognised the name who signed the certificate of authenticity. It sounded familiar. This morning I remembered, a cousin in Florence bought a painting with a counterfeit certificate of authenticity that had the same signature."

Rachele put down the pencil and the notepad.

"That does not mean that the certificate of authenticity you saw last Sunday was not genuine."

"Yes, I know. I wonder if you could discretely find out whether the person who signed it remembers the painting."

Rachele thought about it.

"I would need more information and I might have to involve one of the more senior lawyers or a partner."

"If you do, can you keep it between you and Franco Venier? He is my personal solicitor. I can rely on his keeping matters confidential."

Rachele could not figure out why the count was so careful to keep the whole matter confidential. Then she figured it out.

"Are you concerned that your wife's professional reputation may be irreparably damaged if it becomes known she helped selling a fake, even though she can prove good faith?"

The count smiled and his face lit up. Rachele hoped her husband's face would react in the same way if somebody mentioned her in twenty years.

"It is more than that. I know she gave up her dreams of becoming an artist when she married me, and I am grateful to her. She does not need to work, but it is her way of keeping up with her world and be part of mine. Her reputation is her only professional asset. She would be devastated if she sold a fake, even in good faith. I am prepared to do anything to prevent that."

Rachele closed the notepad. It was her way of hinting that the meeting had ended.

"Let me think of what I can do. I'll send you a note in two days."

The count stood up.

"We can do one better, come to dinner in two days with Gabriele. I will find an excuse to ask your informal opinion on something."

Rachele felt she had to share the conversation with her boss since she probably had to use some of her working hours to investigate whatever she might end up investigating. Franco Venier reassured her Count Pesaro de Bonfili was an old client of the law firm, and had introduced many people who later became good clients; he was more than happy for one of his trainees to do him a favour.

Two days later, Rachele had organised an action plan and was ready to discuss it with the Count before dinner. She and Gabriele arrived early with the excuse that Rachele's boss had given her something he needed to discuss with the count but the count did not have time to go to the law firm. They moved to the count's study while Gabriele was talking to his aunt about why he was leaving the family business to be a civil servant for the City of Venice. By the time Rachele and the count had finished talking about her strategy to find out whether the painting was authentic, other guests had arrived and they were ready to move to the dining room.

Sometimes things just happen. During dinner, one of the other guests asked the countess whether his friend had got in touch with her.

"Yes, he did. He has an authenticated Turner to sell. I thought I knew all the privately owned Turner in the area after I helped curate an exhibition, but that was over ten years ago. I think it was in 1908."

Rachele noticed the other guest's demeanour, and she did not think he was nervous or embarrassed. She concluded he was acting in good faith.

"Well, he might have bought the painting later. I understand that an expert on Turner signed the authentication notice, the one that many owners glue to the back of the painting."

"I have agreed to visit him again in Dolo next week, and then I'll decide whether I can help him. Depending on the whether we shall either take the train or hire a boat. He lives by the Brenta Canal."

"I would hire a boat anytime, so much better than a train, less smoke[1]."

Rachele made a mental note to find a casual way to discuss the painting with the Countess. She had already told the count to write the name of the person who signed the certificate of authenticity. A photograph of the painting would be ideal, but she would think of something else if he could not get one.

The following Monday, Rachele and her boss had finished a meeting discussing a contract that a law firm had to prepare based on the brief of their client. Rachele was collecting her notes and the client brief to prepare the first draft of the contract.

"Do you know anybody who runs an art gallery? I need to figure out what sort of information I need to dispel doubts about the authenticity of a painting. It regards the confidential matter Count Pesaro de Bonfili asked me to look into."

"We have a client that has an art gallery, but how do you plan to keep the matter confidential?"

Rachele smiled

"I simply say that my father is thinking of buying a painting, but a friend doubts its authenticity. For any other information, I am a lawyer. I am trained to keep matters confidential. I am confident I will find a way not to answer questions I am not prepared to answer."

Franco Venier smiled, wrote a name and address, tore the page of the notepad, and gave it to Rachele.

"This art gallery is in Campo San Polo. He is an old client. Tell him I sent you. It may help confidentiality if you do not volunteer, you work for me."

Rachele thanked him and went back to her desk.

Gabriele's parents lived in the last extension of the Ghetto, very close to the synagogues. Saturday lunch at their place was an established tradition. The Pesaro de Bonfilis were frequent guests. Fiamma, Gabriele's mother, and the countess were very close. Myriam Mendes and Sarah Pesaro De Bonfili were born in the same year and had become close friends. If the mothers thought of themselves as honorary sisters, Myriam and Sarah were honorary cousins who got on very well. The family group was walking together to the Mendes's home. Deborah Camerini was talking to Fiamma; her husband told Rachele he knew where to find the information she asked for and would drop by her office during the week once she had them. Rachele thanked him, they were interrupted by Giorgio, his son, and Emanuele Mendes, Gabriele's younger brother, who had been talking to some of their friends at the end of the service and were running to catch up with the rest of the group.

During lunch, Countess Deborah held forth, talking about their trip to Dolo. They had rented a boat and sailed directly to Dolo along the Brenta Canal. It was a nice October day, with a perfect temperature. She also discussed the painting she inspected, a Turner scene of Venice. She liked it, but she was not aware Turner had painted the Rialto bridge. Rachele heard it but did not to look at the count, she was talking to another friend of Gabriele, Alvise Cantoni, who was there with his fiancée. The war had delayed Alvise's studies. He told Rachele he would graduate from Padua Law School a few months later. They joked about starting a law firm together one day.

The following Wednesday, Count Pesaro De Bonfili had a meeting with Franco Venier. He arrived at the law firm ten minutes early and asked to see Rachele.

"When we were at Dolo, I took the time to take some photographs. In the envelope, there are copies of the photograph of the painting and photos of the certificate of authenticity. You can clearly see the name of the person who signed it."

Rachele took the envelope and opened it. The Count added.

"I forgot, there is also a photograph of the letter signed by the vendor, evidence of the provenience of the painting. But I suggest you check the Turner catalogue raisonné. Try the Biblioteca Marciana[2]. Let me know if you can't find it and I'll make enquiries."

Rachele walked with the count to the meeting room where he would have his meeting with Franco Venier

"I'll look at the material and let you know my next steps. I think I'll try to contact the person who signed the certificate of authenticity."

Meanwhile, Franco Venier had arrived for the meeting. Rachele stood up to leave. The count told her to keep him posted. She closed the door of the meeting room and went back to her office.

Rachele took out her notepad and wrote the name of the person who signed the certificate of authenticity. She was thinking of whom to ask, Countess Deborah was the only art dealer she knew in Venice and she could not ask her. Then she realised she did not have to ask somebody in Venice, she only needed to find out in which city that person lived. She could ask her father if he knew an art dealer anywhere in Italy. So she dialled her father's office number in Trieste. A secretary told her to call back in half an hour when her father would be free.

She went to the kitchen and made herself a cup of coffee, before going back to analysing what she thought was an inadequate translation of a contract between one of their clients and a company based in Zurich. The differences between the German text and the Italian text puzzled her. On her way back to her office, she saw Alvise Cantoni talking to the receptionist.

"I did not expect to see you here! Whatever you are here for, please wait until 12.30 when Gabriele comes to walk home with me for our lunch break. He would be very sorry if he missed you."

"I think I am early to talk to Avvocato Venier[3]. Last Shabbat, after lunch at your in-laws, Count Pesaro De Bonfili told me he would introduce me to him."

Rachele smiled. Obviously, Count Pesaro de Bonfili was into matchmaking like his wife, only a different kind of matchmaking.

"Avvocato Venier is my boss. He is in a meeting with Count Pesaro De Bonfili. Do you want a coffee? Come with me. I'll make you one."

She then turns to the receptionist

"Alvise Cantoni will wait for Avvocato Venier in my office. Please let us know when he is available."

Once they were back in her office, Rachele apologised but she had to call her father to see if he had the information she needed for another client. This time Baron Davide Modiano was free.

"Dad, I am sorry, but I need to be quick. I am calling from work. Have you ever heard of an art expert called Adalberto Medici? I need to discuss a certificate of authenticity he signed."

Baron Modiano understood his daughter's haste.

"I think he signed the certificate of authenticity of a painting that is in my study at home. I'll ask the art dealer who sold me the painting and call you back tonight."

"Just one more thing Dad, is the art dealer by any chance Countess Deborah?"

"No, I bought the painting in Florence."

"Thank you, dad, looking forward to talking to you tonight."

After she hung up, Rachele noticed Alvise was not in her office any more. She did not notice him leave.

Chapter Three

November 1921

Once Rachele's father told her Adalberto Medici lived on the shores of Lake Como, she had no problems finding his address and telephone number. She volunteered Gabriele's younger brother, Emanuele, to do the legwork. The other piece that was missing from her search was a copy of the catalogue raisonné of Turner's work, but she planned to ask Mr Medici for help to find it.

She decided to write to him rather than call. Her boss had agreed she could take time to do this during her working hours, but she wanted to minimise the time she used to work at what Count Victor asked her to find out during her working day. She wished Gabriele a good working day at his new job, working for the City he loved so much, and then she took a quick detour to Fondaco dei Tedeschi[1] to post the letter.

The same morning, Rachele received a phone call from her father. He reassured her that everybody was fine. He just wanted to ask her a confidential question.

"Deborah calls me whenever she comes across a painting I might like. I do not buy everything she suggests, but I have sometimes. She brokers private sales and it is cheaper than buying from an art dealer. She contacted me about a Turner painting of Rialto bridge, authenticated by Adalberto Medici. Is this connected with your enquiry?"

Rachele rolled her eyes. She did not need this complication.

"I am afraid it is. This morning I posted a letter to him. Can you not commit to anything until I have a reply? By the way, I know for a fact Countess Deborah is in perfect good faith."

There was a long pause. Rachele could picture her father's thinking face.

"I know. She only works with people she knows, but I also know that sometimes it is not enough. I am happy you are investigating. Happy for her and for me."

Rachele smiled

"I think Count Victor asked for my help because there is something that bothers him."

A week later, she received a letter from Adalberto Medici. He had provided a lot if information. His last paragraph was not what Rachele hoped to read:

"Thank you for enclosing a photograph of the painting. I never saw it. Please compare my signature with the signature of the certificate of authenticity. Since you are already involved, I am thinking of travelling to Venice to engage your law firm to protect my name. I wonder how many others fake certificates of authenticity are out there."

Adalberto Medici enclosed his phone numbers and asked her to get in touch with him.

Rachele's first reaction was to look for Franco Venier. She needed to know if she could sign up a client for the law firm.

Then, she rang Adalberto Medici, who confirmed he had never seen the painting.

"That does not mean it is not authentic; I cannot have an opinion until I see the painting. I never authenticated it. How did your law firm become involved?"

Rachele chose to be diplomatic and vague.

"The owner hired an art broker to sell the painting, her husband had a gut feeling and asked us to investigate."

Adalberto Medici surprised her.

"If the gut feeling comes from another painting I allegedly authenticated, I need to talk to you. I will write to you this evening once I have made plans to come to Venice. Can you please give me another call once you have received the letter? I would like to make an appointment to discuss this matter."

Rachele knew she had to follow the firm's protocol.

"A secretary might be in touch to arrange an appointment."

Rachele continued the conversation for as long as her manners allowed her before she said goodbye and hung up. She then talked to her boss about Adalberto Medici. Her boss congratulated her.

"You have been here for a month and you already have sorted out problems in a bilingual contract and you may have secured a new client for the firm. Maybe I will win this bet."

Rachele smiled

"Which bet?"

Franco Venier grinned from ear to ear.

"The one you told me about before I hired you. "

"Thank you. Now I have to call Count Victor to tell him about the letter I received. Do we know of an expert who can show us why the signature in the certificate of authenticity could not be authentic? Pun intended."

"Why do you need that?"

Rachele was ready

"We now know that Adalberto Medici never saw the painting. We need to establish if somebody falsified the signature or lifted the certificate of authenticity from another painting and changed the description. If we end up preparing a fraud case to present to the police, we have to be precise."

Franco Venier kept his grin.

"I have most definitely won the bet!"

Rachele went back to her office feeling happy. She knew that a married woman practising law was not common and was grateful to her boss for hiring her. It was a great boost to her morale to know Franco Venier was satisfied with her work. She now had to call Count Victor, a conversation she was not eager to have. She kept the initial social chat to a minimum and came to the point.

"Adalberto Medici has no memory of ever seeing the painting. He is even coming to Venice to talk to us to file a civil lawsuit against whomever is abusing his hard-earned excellent reputation. Now, how well do you know the seller?"

Count Pesaro de Bonfili took some time before responding

"I would like to give him the benefit of the doubt. He gave Deborah the letter from the collector who sold him the painting. He must have known that she would check. For the moment, let us assume he is in good faith. What is the next step?"

Rachele was ready

"Besides telling your wife?"

Rachele could not see the smile on Count Pesaro de Bonfili's face. He had a plan.

"I was thinking of inviting you and Gabriele to dinner to try the fish restaurant that opened a month ago near the Ghetto. Then we tell her. What else we can do?"

Rachele could see why Count Victor thought there was strength in numbers.

"My suggestion is to wait until we speak to Adalberto Medici. We need to establish who falsified the credentials to sell a fake Turner. I would love to accept your invitation. I need to ask Gabriele, but I think you should tell your wife beforehand. She may not be happy to find out we knew and did not tell her as soon as we found out."

She failed to convince Count Victor.

"If we tell her in a public place, her innate manners will prevent her from exploding."

Rachele laughed and promised to call him the following day after she had discussed it with Gabriele.

Franco Venier had said many times that Mr. Medici would be Rachele's client. She did not expect to sign up a new client two months into her new job. She had to be prepared and confident. Her nerves and her care for details were a great help. Photographs of the painting, the certificate of authenticity, and the letter from the person who sold the painting to the current seller were spread on her desk; her notepad was full of notes. Count Pesaro de Bonfili was supposed to arrive half an hour into the meeting and Franco Venier would show their new prospect around the law firm while Rachele welcomed her honorary uncle before the second part of the meeting started.

Adalberto Medici was not familiar with Venice. The hotel had given him precise instruction how to reach the office of the law firm, but he got lost. Luckily, his plan to walk around the Rialto market on the other side of the Grand Canal gave him enough time to find his way again and be on time. He valued punctuality.

Rachele believed in being prepared, she had a folder with photographs and notes and another one with all the paperwork a new client would have to sign. She was already in the meeting room when the receptionist walked in with Mr. Medici. He reminded Rachele of one of her father clients from London when she was a teenager. They made small talk while they were waiting for refreshments. Once they drank their coffee, Rachele summarised the situation.

"We know you never saw the painting before, so you could not have authenticated it. We also have established that they did not alter a certificate of authenticity of another painting because the expert we consulted compared the signature in the certificate with the signature in your letter and showed us where the two differ. He also proved that the same person who falsified your signature wrote the description of the painting. We need to investigate the previous sellers until we can establish the origin of the painting."

Although they had spoken on the phone, Adalberto Medici did not expect that "Avvocato Modiano" was a woman. However, he liked how thorough Rachele had been in establishing the situation.

"I need to find out whether there are other false authentications in the market and would welcome your help in drafting a statement I can use to separate myself from them, I also need your advice whether it makes sense to go to court on this matter."

"What do you mean? The forger committed a crime, once we have evidence we need to submit it to the police. If they agree with us, they will question everybody involved in this and they will take it to court. The choice may not be yours."

"I meant going to court to protect my name."

Rachele wrote 'Protect his name' in her notes and told him they would consider it once they have more evidence. Maybe a carefully drafted article in a newspaper would be enough. Mr. Medici was a victim of a fraudster just as much as those who bought, or sold, a fake painting in good faith.

Half an hour into the meeting Franco Venier walked into the room, Rachele introduced him to Mr Medici then informed her client that Count Pesaro de Bonfili was due in five minutes. Avvocato Venier would show him around and discuss the law firm term while she updated Count Pesaro de Bonfili on a separate matter, then she would introduce him and the meeting would continue. In the meantime, her uncle had arrived, and she updated him. The meeting continued once her boss and her first client joined them. Rachele introduced her honorary uncle, then she came straight to the point.

"Mr. Medici, I have asked Count Pesaro De Bonfili to join us because he asked me in confidence to verify the authenticity of the certificate. He had more than a gut feeling. He remembered a cousin in Florence buying a painting with your certificate of authenticity that turned out to be false."

Adalberto Medici interrupted

"In the art world, nobody is infallible. I might have believed in good faith that a painting was authentic."

Rachele cut him off.

"Nobody questions your good faith, Mr. Medici. Anyway, we owe it to the count's hunch if we established that the certificate of authenticity of the painting allegedly by Turner that Deborah Camerini examined in Dolo was forged. I think that Count Pesaro De Bonfili can assist us in the investigation in figuring out who is behind this and take it to court or deliver the evidence to the police, depending on the outcome."

Alberto Medici felt chastised, apologised, and picked up the pen, ready to continue taking notes. Rachele continued.

"Our next step would be to investigate the art dealer or the private collection who sold the painting to the acquaintance of the Pesaro de Bonfilis. I asked the count to join us because it might be necessary for him to go back to his cousin and ask where he bought the painting allegedly authenticated by you."

The two men looked at each other; Count Victor was the faster to ask what was on both their minds.

"I have no problem with that, but why?"

Rachele opened her notepad, went back a couple of pages.

"Let us assume for a minute that you are both my clients. Mr. Medici, I know you have signed nothing yet and you may decide not to proceed with us, but, for the moment, the assumption will make explaining my ideas much easier."

Adalberto Medici nodded. He had already decided to hire the service of this surprising young woman.

"I have already established what the Count asked me to find out. The Turner has a counterfeit certificate of authenticity glued in the back of the frame. There are many questions and the Count may decide to continue working with me on the matter, but the subject is closed. However, his case brought us to you. You want to protect your reputation, and that is a wider issue."

Rachele paused, as if she were presenting a case in court. Adalberto Medici used her pause to reinforce the importance of his reputation.

"This is my principal asset. If there is a doubt about my honesty, my professional life is over."

Rachele continued, trying very hard not to sound patronising or annoyed because she was interrupted.

"Quite so, to achieve your goal, we need to find the forger or the way paintings enter the art market with a forged certificate of authenticity. For the moment, I assume that the letter written by the seller of the fake Turner to the count's acquaintance is genuine, but I am keeping an open mind."

The count was watching the recent addition to his wife's honorary family full of avuncular pride. His niece had a brilliant mind, determination, and focus. No wonder she finished University despite the hostility around her being the only woman in her year to study law.

"Therefore, Mr. Medici, if you decide to hire us, I will ask Count Pesaro De Bonfili to ask his cousin where he bought the painting and establish where his acquaintance bought the fake Turner. If they come from the same place, we have a starting point to collect evidence to give to the police."

Adalberto Medici was impressed.

"I am happy with term and conditions and the cost discussed with Avvocato Venier. You are a very impressive young woman. I have every confidence you will protect my name and reputation."

Rachele thanked Count Pesaro De Bonfili, she excused herself with Mr Medici saying that she would see her client out and come back with the firm's bookkeeper to complete the paperwork to sign him as a client. The receptionist brought Count Victor his coat. He hugged Rachele.

"I am proud of you. Once I am back in my office, I'll call your father. I want to tell him how impressive and confident you were. Davide will be proud of you."

"Count Victor, in reality, I was very nervous. Adalberto Medici would be the first client I sign."

"Then I am even more proud of you."

He hugged her and gave her an avuncular kiss on her forehead, adding that he was sure that was what her father would have done if he had been in the meeting. Rachele asked the receptionist to tell the bookkeeper to join them in the meeting room and re-joined Adalberto Medici.

"So, what is the next step once I have taken care of the paperwork?"

"Do you have contacts in newspapers? If you are in Venice for the next two nights, I shall prepare a statement by tomorrow afternoon. If that meets your approval, we shall organise as many copies as the number of newspapers and magazines you want it to appear. You will then share with us the name and address of somebody in those publications that can either write an article about your statement or get the statement published. I just have one request, if you agree."

"What is it?"

"Can we just keep it generic? Count Pesaro De Bonfili's acquaintance has not been informed yet that the certificate of authenticity attached to his painting is a forgery."

"Of course, I have no problems with that."

Rachele organised a second meeting for the following afternoon, left Adalberto Medici in the capable hands of the bookkeeper, and went looking for her boss. A huge grin on her face.

"He is signing. I have secured my first client."

Franco Venier lifted his head from whatever he was reading.

"He told me he had a lot of doubts when he found out that

Avvocato Modiano was a woman, but you impressed him. He thought he had come to the right place. I have won my bet!"

Rachele smiled. The adrenaline had left her body. She took a detour to the kitchen for a much-needed cup of coffee and bumped into Alvise Cantoni.

"What are you doing here?"

"I was waiting for you. Franco Venier has just hired me hourly to do some research work until I graduate. Sometimes I want to take a break from writing my thesis."

"Welcome, Gabriele will be happy for you. Join me for a coffee. I just signed my first client."

Alvise smiled

"Congratulations to the woman of the hour. The person who was showing me around heard the way your client talked about you and how your boss reacted. Gabriele will be very proud."

Rachele blushed as she was making coffee.

Rachele had invited her parents-in-law to dine at the restaurant with her husband and her uncle and aunt. She thought Fiamma would have a calming effect on her close friend once she was told that Adalberto Medici never saw the painting and therefore the certificate of authenticity was false. Deborah Camerini thought that her nephew and niece would tell them that Rachele was expecting a baby. Her husband knew why they were there and was silently hoping that the restaurant would survive the evening.

Dinner had been very good and the conversation was pleasant. Rachele decided to wait until after dessert were eaten, when she discussed it with Count Pesaro De Bonfili he had made a joke about all knives having been removed from the table by that time.

"Aunt Deborah, there is something I need to tell you."

Countess Pesaro de Bonfili was expecting something like that, her grin was wider than her face. Rachele knew she would disappoint her.

"I met with Adalberto Medici this afternoon, he confirmed that he never saw the Turner and therefore cannot have signed the certificate of authenticity. You cannot rely on it to establish the authenticity of the painting."

The grin faded very quickly in Deborah Camerini's face. However, the ploy of telling her in a public place had worked. Those who knew her noticed that she had straightened up her posture, closed her eyes, and raised her head. She was clearly controlling herself. She turned to her husband, her voice apparently calm but very cold

"Do you think Giorgio Baldan knew?"

Gabriele could see the metaphorical icicles coming out of his aunt's mouth. He checked for any sharp object on the table and noticed his mother had stood up and moved behind her close friends, her hands on Deborah's shoulders to help her control her temper. Her husband expected a similar reaction.

"I do not see why he could possibly have known."

Rachele felt she had to come to her uncle's rescue

"Adalberto Medici said the forger imitated his signature very well."

The countess seemed to have relaxed. Fiamma moved back to her seat but she was holding her friend's hand as if she could absorb some of her friend's temper. Samuele whispered in his son's ear

"Inviting Mum and I as well was a very smart move."

Gabriele whispered back.

"My wife is a very smart woman."

The countess had been looking at Rachele and her husband, she took a deep breath.

"Rachele, don't worry! I am not going to shoot the messenger. However, we need to go immediately because I need to figure out what I am going to tell to those I contacted about the Turner. I am going to have a very difficult day tomorrow."

She stood up, they all stood up. She went to get her coat, followed by her husband. Rachele had the opportunity to wish good luck to her uncle.

Fiamma and Samuele left with the Pesaro De Bonfilis, on their way across the bridge on the Rio della Misericordia, Deborah turned to her friend

"When I saw you, I thought Rachele was going to tell us she was expecting."

Chapter Four

November 1921

R achele was visiting her aunt Deborah. She needed to check if what she had in mind made sense. Helping friends buy and sell art was a hobby for Deborah Camerini. She enjoyed doing it, but did not need the money. However, Rachele soon found out that the countess was very respected in the art world and not just in Italy.

They were in the Pesaro De Bonfili smaller, intimate, blue sitting room, reserved for friends and family. That afternoon the dowager countess, Deborah's mother-in-law, was receiving her friends more formally in the larger sitting room, called the red sitting room, from the colour of the upholstery.

Countess Pesaro De Bonfili was proud of her niece. Rachele might have become part of her clan after she married Gabriele Mendes, but the countess had known her ever since she was born. Her husband and Rachele's father were business acquaintances who became very close friends. The Countess loved holding forth. She was describing the checks she was making before accepting to sell a painting or suggesting to a client to buy a specific painting.

"A painting should bring you joy, but buying a painting is like seeing through reflections in the water on a sunny day. You need to be careful that the reflection of the sun does not blind you from noticing details. As you found out, the devil is in the detail. In your case, you need to go back to a common entry point, a person or an art gallery that sold many of the paintings with a counterfeit certificate of authenticity."

Earlier, Rachele had closed the notepad to enjoy the refreshments.

"My idea was to see if we could find a common source for the six paintings we know have forged certificates. The irony is that Adalberto Medici reviewed one of those paintings and in his opinion it was authentic. He has prepared another certificate of authenticity with a notarised stamp. A shame it is not the alleged Turner."

The Countess was pouring more tea into their cups.

"It makes sense, but to do that, you need either a paper trail or the cooperation of the buyer. It can be difficult when you have a long chain. For instance, your father bought many paintings I suggested. The way I work, he bought them from me and I bought them from the seller. In this example, you would have to contact your father and me. It can become a bit time-consuming."

Rachele put down the teacup and picked up her notepad. She found the page she wanted fairly quickly.

"Our researcher, Alvise Cantoni, will travel to an art dealer in Florence who appears in three chains; again, unfortunately not the alleged Turner. If he does not find any further origin for the painting, we may have the evidence we are looking for."

"I did not know that you were so far ahead. Why did you not come to me earlier?"

"It was a matter of finding the time. I did not want to use evenings or weekends. It is not urgent and I do not discuss business on Shabbat. But thank you for explaining how you work. It helped me get into the mindset of an art broker and we may go further with our evidence."

The Countess took a sip from her cup of tea. The conversation was coming to its natural end.

"What do you hope to achieve?"

Rachele stood up.

"We need to build a credible case for a civil lawsuit. Avvocato Venier reckons that if we find four paintings with a forged certificate of authenticity coming from the same source, we have a strong enough civil case. If we find firm evidence of who the forger might be, we give everything to the police and ask them to mention our clients as a major help in their investigation to stop a major forger."

Rachele thought she had spent time alone with a countess without her making any comment about her. Her honorary aunt could murder somebody with a polite phrase. She had not reckoned with Deborah Camerini's parting comments when she was seeing her out.

"I am very proud of you. You are becoming more and more confident and more and more elegant every time I see you. You and Gabriele must come to dinner one Friday night. I'll be in touch to organise a date."

Once she was walking to the waterbus stop, she realised she had not seen the dowager countess. She wondered whether her aunt Deborah and her mother-in-law led separate social lives. She made a mental note to ask Fiamma, Gabriele's mother.

Rachele and Franco Venier were discussing the Adalberto Medici case. In Rachele's opinion, they had enough circumstantial evidence to start a case against an art dealer who was in the chain of ownership of six paintings that had a proven, forged certificate of authenticity. Her boss was looking at Rachele's summary. He was impressed but had a few questions.

"So, Adalberto Medici never saw any of those paintings, and you can prove that the signature on the forged certificate is not his. So, we have six proven false paintings?"

Rachele corrected her boss

"We have one painting Adalberto Medici and another expert think it is authentic, from Monet by the way, and five paintings of dubious origin."

Franco Venier stood up and started pacing the room.

"For our reputation, we need to make sure we have the best possible case and protect our client from risking time and money in a case he cannot win. So, how did we collect that information?"

Rachele was ready. She looked at her notes. Thirty people had written to them following the four articles written based on the statement they had prepared. Mr Medici could confirm that he signed 20 of those certificates of authenticity, but ten were of dubious origin. Five of the owners of paintings with dubious certificates co-operated. Franco Venier mentally congratulated himself for hiring this unconventional young woman. Rachele had not finished.

"Alvise Cantoni helped me trace the chain of ownership of those paintings and of the alleged Turner, the same art dealer in Siena who appears in all of them. Our case is only on the forgery of certificates of authenticity. We are not making any claim on the actual authenticity of those paintings."

Franco Venier laughed

"You have not worked with us for two months and you already have an assistant."

Rachele smiled back and replied in an innocent tone.

"Well, he offered. He needed a diversion from writing his thesis."

Other lawyers had teased Franco Venier because he had hired a woman. He wished they were all in his office now. Somebody was having the last laugh, and it was not them. He was more and more impressed by the mind and the ability of the young woman they teased him for hiring.

"So what do we advise Mr Medici?"

"I think we have enough evidence for a civil case against the art dealer in Siena. At least we write him a strong letter asking for the origin of the paintings and if he does not provide an acceptable answer, we send another letter asking for damages. I also suggest we ask Mr Medici's consent to give all the evidence we found to the police for a criminal case. It will be their problem figuring out if the art dealer in Siena did not want to pay for expertise or if he knowingly introduced fake paintings into the market."

"I am very impressed. By the way, Adalberto Medici looked at the paperwork he signed almost a month after he signed it. He wrote to me asking to remove my name as his leading solicitor. He wants yours."

"Should I write him thanking him but asking him to agree to leave your name?"

"Absolutely not! I will brag about you with all my peers who laughed at my decision to hire a woman."

Rachele blushed and stood up. When she got to the door, she turned back to face her boss.

"Well, I am happy I provided the reason for your last laugh!"

~

Deborah Camerini and Fiamma Andrade met when they were six. They became friends, and they grew closer and closer. They had brothers but longed for a sister and became each other's sister. When Debora's mother died in 1883, when they were ten, Fiamma's mother emotionally adopted Deborah. By the time they had children, their children called the other one aunt. During the early days of Gabriele and Rachele's relationship, he told her he figured that Countess Deborah Pesaro De Bonfili was only an honorary aunt when he was fifteen.

The two families were used to having Shabbat lunch all together every other Saturday. Fiamma did not trust Deborah's mother-in-law's adherence to Jewish dietary rules, so lunch at the Pesaro De Bonfili was fish-based. The Pesaro De Bonfili's cook would call Fiamma to discuss recipes, so she would always feel comfortable eating what she had on her plate. Lunch at the Mendeses was easier and more relaxed, Deborah Camerini was seldom relaxed around her mother-in-law.

Wherever they had lunch, after the first course, the countess would stand up and toast somebody. It was a very theatrical performance, but the two honorary sisters were following a tradition started by Fiamma's mother. Somebody around that table would be congratulated, praised, and made to feel the star of the moment. After Fiamma died, when she was 90, the family found a notebook with dates and names. They figured out that the two honorary sisters kept notes of whom they had celebrated to make sure that everybody was praised with the same frequency.

The Saturday after Rachele filed the civil suit, Deborah stood up

"I would like to toast our star of the Venetian legal world, Rachele Modiano Mendes. Not only she has officially been assigned a client after less than two months in her job, but she is supposed to present the case at trial. I have it from a reputable source."

By now Rachele had been through enough of those ceremonies to know that she had to stand and take a bow while everybody was applauding. Count Pesaro De Bonfili added to her embarrassment, saying that he called her father to tell him, just in case. He then whispered to Samuele, Fiamma's husband, that Rachele's parents were planning to come to Venice to watch their daughters in court, but she was not supposed to know.

Chapter Five

November 1921

Rachele loved Venice in the fog, at least when the fog was not so thick to hide everything around her. Everything looked out of focus as she left her home, walking to work alongside her husband. She enjoyed looking at her surroundings, trusting Gabriele's ability to find the way. When they reached the top of the Rialto bridge, they stopped for her usual 'Canaletto Moment'. Looking at the Grand Canal had not grown old yet, six months after her permanent move to Venice.

"Somehow, it feels like the buildings are asleep. "

Gabriele looked at his wife and smiled. She could have read entries in a directory and he would have smiled. He felt he was walking on air just being next to her.

"One building is going to have a rude awakening. This morning I have to finish looking at an application for maintenance work for one of those buildings."

They started walking again. Rachele was clinging to her husband because the steps felt slippery. Maybe she was wearing the wrong shoes. They both enjoyed the closeness.

Once they reached Rachele's office, Gabriele kissed his wife on the cheek and wished her a good morning in the office.

As she was taking off her coat, she noticed a thick envelope with a Siena postmark on her desk. She guessed it was from the art dealer who sold paintings with the forged certificate of authenticity. They only had investigated six of the twenty that had emerged from the articles written about the statement they prepared on behalf of Adalberto Medici. He has sold all six of them.

Still with her coat on, she went looking for Franco Venier's secretary and asked if her boss had some free time later in the morning. She walked to her office looking at the letter, expecting some sort of defensive argument. The art dealer had written something else. Later, her boss agreed she had to ask her client to come to Venice. The next step could only happen with Mr Medici's consent.

That evening, Gabriele and Rachele had agreed to babysit for Gabriele's closest friends Paolo and Sofia Mondani. Paolo's decision to marry his fiancé before he and Gabriele were called to fight in World War I had been controversial. He was a medical student and could have got a deferral, but became a medic in the Italian Army and deferred his studies. He insisted on marrying his fiancée before being sent to the front line. Their son, Arrigo, was born nine months after a three-day licence after he finished army training. His wife would point out that their son was born in February 1918, 12 months after they got married.

Paolo and Sofia came back from their walk. Gabriele and Rachele spent some time with their friends and then left. On their way home, Rachele brought up the subject of children.

"My mother used to say, children come when they come. The more you want them, the less likely you are to have them. I think Franco Venier will not fire me if I become pregnant, but

I hope we have a housekeeper before our first child arrives. It would be a tremendous help in managing everything."

Rachele had surprised her husband, but Gabriele liked the idea that his wife was thinking of children after spending some time with Arrigo.

"I think we can afford a live-in housekeeper, but I would rather sit down with you and look at our income before we start looking. Just in case we have a baby before we find her, couldn't Maria help?"

Rachele felt she was a lucky woman. Few men would have had no problems with their wives working once they had a child. And she did not even have to. Gabriele's income was more than enough.

"Maria comes every morning and has her own family. She can't step in if we have to work late or if one of us has to travel for work."

They had reached the end of Calle del Tentor, they climbed the first flight of steps to cross the bridge over a narrow canal. Once they were on top, Gabriele put an arm around his wife's shoulders and looked at her under the light of a lamp so he could swim in her green eyes.

"All right, tomorrow lunchtime we have a grilled fish somewhere in a restaurant near your office, and look at how much we earn."

"I hate to spoil the moment, but tomorrow morning, I have a tough day. I need to tell Adalberto Medici that his case has become more complicated. Can we have that conversation at home after work? Mr Medici is not staying in Venice tomorrow night, so I am bound to finish at a decent time."

Gabriele had an idea

"If you can leave early, why don't you meet me outside my

office and then we have a pre-dinner drink somewhere, maybe even dinner?"

They had now crossed the second bridge before Campo San Giacomo dall'Orio. They were almost home.

"You know, after about six months in Venice, I still find it very romantic walking at night with you by my side."

For the second time that evening, Gabriele looked at his wife and felt like he was swimming in her green eyes.

"I have lived in Venice all my life and I still find it very romantic. Let's be romantic together."

The following morning, Rachele surprised her husband when Gabriele woke up. She was ready to leave for work. It was an important day for her and she wanted time to prepare. She had to explain all the alternatives to her only client. She did not want a frustrated Mr Medici to go to her boss and complain, even if the complaint was not justified.

Adalberto Medici had decided that there were advantages to working with a Venetian based lawyer. He could turn a business trip into a brief holiday in Venice. He had arrived two days earlier with his wife. The hotel had arranged for his wife to visit the Mendes workshop, during the morning he was going to spend at the law firm. He did not know that the silk merchant was the family business of his lawyer's in-laws. He had breakfast with his wife, met her guide for the morning, and walked to Calle de l'Aquila Nera, wondering why his lawyer wanted to meet him in person.

When Rachele entered the meeting room, she found him standing by the window trying to position himself to get a glimpse of the bridge or the Grand Canal.

"If you want a glimpse of the Grand Canal, you need to stand about twenty centimetres away from the window on the other side. You can only see two steps of the Rialto bridge. Good morning and welcome back to Venice."

Adalberto Medici was in his own personal world, so Rachele's voice surprised him. He turned around with a concerned face, almost as if his lawyer had caught him red-handed doing something naughty. He recovered and greeted Rachele and the receptionist, who had followed Rachele into the meeting room to take orders for refreshments.

Once that was out of the way, Rachele set down and started taking documents out of a folder.

"We had a letter from the art dealer in Siena. He claims he bought all the paintings from an estate somewhere on the Riviera del Brenta. They all came with a certificate of authenticity. He has asked his accountant to retrieve two years old paperwork. This is an important development."

She passed on the letter to Adalberto Medici, who started reading it.

"Why?"

"We were working under the assumption that we would collect evidence for a court case, or a settlement, against the art dealer. If the documentation he gives us is a hundred per cent reliable, he can prove his good faith. He had no reason to believe that someone had falsified those certificates. You have a name, which we aim to protect. He trusted your name. All the twenty signatures looked authentic. "

Mr Medici put down the letter.

"But if you compare it to anything I have written, you can see that the letter d in Adalberto and Medici differs from anything I wrote."

Rachele hoped not to sound patronising.

"Absolutely, but until an expert calligrapher pointed out the differences, I could not see it. I do not think that an eye that is not thinking someone might have forged the signature could spot the differences between the letter d in those signatures and anything you have written."

"So, what do we do now?"

Rachele went through all the options, including doing nothing. In the end, she presented her strategy.

"We involve the police. Initially, we could ask them to open a criminal case against unknown individuals for fraud and art forgery. We wait for the art dealer to come back to us with the details of the estate and we retrieve a copy of the will, if there is a will, otherwise I hope there is a name of a notary in the document the art dealer will send us. Based on what we find, we see what the police make of it all and we join the criminal proceeding as a civil party seeking damages."

Adalberto Medici was silent for what Rachele thought was a long time.

"I have no problem with that, but let's wait to decide until we have the paperwork from the art dealer in Siena."

That was more or less what Rachele hoped to hear. There was something else she felt they had to know before they could make an informed decision.

"There is one other thing I think we ought to do once we have the paperwork. Wills are public. I would like to check if the will has a list of paintings, and how they are described."

Rachele could see the question mark on Adalberto Medici's face.

"We have established there are twenty instances of your forged signature. We can trace six of them back to the same

46

source. One of them is a real Monet. Let's take the Turner, for instance, if it is described in the will as a Turner, the deceased owner was in good faith and the executor of the estate or somebody else might have put the forged certificate of authenticity in the back of the painting. If the will does not describe it as a Turner, we may have something more complicated in our hands, and I suggest we let the police investigate."

Adalberto Medici needed little time to think about it.

"All right, let me know when you receive the letter and let's plan another meeting at a date that would allow you to investigate the will. Then we meet and discuss what to do next."

That was what Rachele wanted to hear. The meeting had gone well and had been shorter than she expected. Franco Venier was walking past the meeting room when they were wrapping up and joined them to say hello.

Once she had seen Mr Medici out, Rachele went looking for her boss to update him and ask if she could leave an hour early.

Rachele and Gabriele had treated themselves to afternoon drinks at Caffe Florian. The tourist season was over so there were few people sitting in the café, it was private enough to have a conversation about what they could afford to pay a housekeeper and whom to ask if it was enough to have a choice of candidates for a live-in position. Rachele had taken a notepad out of her briefcase and had written the details of their financials, and added the salary they agreed they could afford to pay at the end of the page. She doubled underline it, closed the notepad, put it back in her briefcase, and put her handbag inside the briefcase as well. They left the café and started walking towards the vaporetto stop on their way home. They were an unusual couple. A man and a woman with matching briefcases were a rare sight in 1921 Venice.

Chapter Six

Rachele had received the paperwork from Carlo Simoni, the art dealer in Siena. She now knew the details of the estate that sold him a few paintings. She made an appointment to talk to the notary, the official solicitor who dealt with the will, and asked to see a copy. Alvise was three weeks away from graduation, but he agreed to go to the notary before his final push with his thesis. When he came back with interesting news, he barged into Rachele's office without knocking. Rachele was examining another international contract where her fluency in German was an asset for the whole firm. She lifted her head from the desk as she heard the noise of the door being slammed open, looked at Alvise, who said nothing, sat down, and took a list out of his briefcase.

"These are the paintings listed in the will. There is no specific mention of anything else. The list is pretty detailed, down to the number of glasses. There is also an addendum stating the number of broken plates or glasses, or any damaged item."

Rachele looked at the list.

"Are you sure you copied everything?"

Alvise sat upright and tried to relax.

"I checked four times."

Rachele looked at the list again.

"But there are only four paintings listed here!"

Alvise was sure.

"I even cross-referenced it with the list we received from Mr Simoni and the list of forged certificates of authenticity that we compiled following the articles about Adalberto Medici betrayed good faith."

Rachele put a bookmark in the contract, closed it, and compared the two lists herself.

"If I remember correctly, only two of the four are on the list of paintings we investigated. Adalberto Medici declared one authentic. The other one is a Josef Hoffman, and the owner is paying for an expert in the Secession movement in Vienna to authenticate it because it looked authentic to our client, but he is not an expert in the Secession movement."

Alvise could see that Rachele was slowly reaching the same conclusions he had reached. Rachele opened a drawer of her desk and retrieved the folder marked Medici-Pesaro De Bonfili. She checked the list of paintings.

"Let us limit ourselves to the six we followed. Where do the other four come from? How did they end up on the list of paintings purchased by Carlo Simoni in 1919?"

Alvise had another surprise for her

"I think you should show Carlo Simoni's list to your honorary aunt."

"Why?"

"If I remember correctly a conversation we had at your in-laws one Shabbat lunch, the last name of the executor might explain my suggestion."

Rachele went back to the list that Alvise had copied from the original will and sat there speechless for a couple of minutes.

"The last name is the same as the last name of the friend who suggested that Aunt Deborah be involved in the sale of the alleged Turner. By the way, the Turner painting is even closer to me; my father was thinking of buying it."

Alvise was too excited to leave, but he really had to work on his thesis.

"I need to go now, but I think you need to discuss with Avvocato Venier how a list of four became a list of 12, and where the remaining eight come from."

"And we need to decide how to present this to our client, let alone figure out what we should advise him to do. Thank you Alvise, I will keep you posted."

She stood up to see him out, then went back to her office, picked up the phone and asked to be connected to Count Pesaro De Bonfili's office. She was too excited not to come straight to the point.

"Uncle Victor, there is an interesting development in the case of the forged certificate of authenticity. I would like to discuss it with you in private before the family hears about it. When can you come to the office?"

Count Pesaro De Bonfili agreed to drop by towards the end of their working day.

Rachele had to go back to her contract and also wanted a distraction from the forged certificates case. She was a firm believer in the power of the back of her mind. Concentrating on something else would help her. She asked her boss's secretary to book her an hour with Franco Venier after lunch,

51

not later than four pm, because Count Pesaro De Bonfili would come to see her sometimes after five.

That day, her in-laws had invited her and Gabriele to lunch. When she saw her husband walking towards her from Campo San Bartolomeo, she decided not to discuss her morning, beyond telling him she saw Alvise. They walked towards Fondamenta del Ghetto, where Gabriele's parents lived. The conversation was all about Gabriele's day. When he asked her about her morning, she simply told him it was very intense and she needed to step away from it for a couple of hours.

During the week, the family used the back door. The front door was the door to the office and the showroom, with all the samples of printed silk made from the warehouse nearby. Gabriele rang the bell to announce their arrival, but let them in with his set of keys. They did not expect to see Arrigo Modiano running towards them shouting 'Uncle Gabriele', closely followed by Myriam, Gabriele's sister, who caught him before he risked falling off the stairs.

"Paolo has an exam this morning and Sofia's mother has a hospital appointment in Padua, so Mum volunteered to take care of Arrigo for the day. "

Rachele knew Fiamma would mention children and look at them during lunch. She picked up Arrigo gave him a kiss on the cheek and told him he was a big boy and should pay attention to steps.

Fiamma was even more subtle than Rachele thought. She simply asked if they had made any progress with hiring a housekeeper. Rachele had shared with her the plan to wait to have a trusted live-in housekeeper before they had children. Gabriele told her that the woman recommended by her brother would start on January 2nd.

Lunch was the break from her thoughts Rachele needed. She forgot about the contract, the forged certificates of authenticity, and her office for an hour and a half. She was back a little late but was planning to finish late. Her meeting with Count Pesaro De Bonfili could last quite a while and she had work to do afterwards.

She was trying to summarise the case of the forged certificates of authenticity. She decided that the case was complex enough to use the system of diagrams one of her University professors used.

She drew one circle and wrote the name of the estate inside it and the name of the executor, then another one and wrote the name of Carlo Simoni in it. A line connected the two. She wrote 'Four paintings became twelve. When did that happen?'

Another circle had the name of Adalberto Medici in it, and then she added, 'Who organised the forged certificates of authenticity?' to the right of the circle.

Those were the core questions that needed to be answered. She then wrote bullet points of possible next steps based on what the answers to those questions might be.

1. If it had been a case of somebody falsifying paintings and then attaching a false certificate of authenticity to them, the police had to be involved. The Monet and the Hoffman made her wonder whether the false certificates of authenticity were a diversion to pass fake paintings as authentic. If Count Victor had not asked her to investigate the alleged Turner, the person who had the idea to falsify Adalberto Medici's signature might have got away with it.

2. What could be the reason for using counterfeit certificates of authenticity on authentic paintings? Time pressure to sell them? Here, the art dealer could have asked somebody else to write them, she had already organised an expert calligrapher to check his

handwritten letter, and he had ruled out Carlo Simoni to be the writer of the false certificates, but he could still have commissioned them. Anybody else? Maybe the one who thought to multiply the number of paintings owned by the deceased?

3. If somebody connected with settling the estate of the deceased multiplied the number of paintings, when did that happen? Was it an isolated case, an opportunity seized at the right time, or were there others? Even in this case, the police had to be involved.

Rachele was ready for the meeting with her boss. She looked at her watch. Her timing was impeccable.

Franco Venier agreed they could just send an update to Adalberto Medici, but it was pointless to ask him to come to Venice until they had a vague idea of who could be behind the multiplication of the number of paintings in the inventory associated with the will. He also pointed out how they could find out. Alvise saw a typewritten inventory. Carlo Simoni sent them a photograph of a handwritten list. Maybe finding who wrote that list, might bring them a step closer to figuring out who multiplied the number of paintings. Franco Venier had a friend who magistrate at the Venetian court. He could ask him for advice.

Rachele was ready to talk to her uncle. Count Pesaro de Bonfili arrived at the law firm at half past five. After a few minutes of family conversation centred around the following Saturday lunch, Rachele came to the point.

"We have established that an art dealer from Siena, Carlo Simoni, sold the Turner and other paintings with the falsified certificate of authenticity. He bought them from the sale of a villa near Mira belonging to a deceased aristocrat with heirs living outside Italy."

Count Pesaro de Bonfili was listening, but Rachele could read the big question mark on his face.

"I asked you to meet me at work because I need your advice on a very delicate matter. The executor of the will was Stefano Baldan."

The question mark on Count Victor's face turned into a concerned look.

"You mean the brother of Giorgio Baldan, the friend who suggested that Deborah might help a friend of his sell a Turner?"

Rachele was happy she did not have to explain or insinuate anything.

"Exactly. We seem to have come back to where we started from. I am not making any assumption but I wondered if you could help arrange a meeting with Stefano Baldan. I hope to borrow your manners and your tact to do that, without creating a drama or causing suspicion."

Count Pesaro De Bonfili smiled, and looked at his niece with pride in his eyes, but was not in a good mood.

"I can see your mother in the way you are approaching this problem. Admittedly, it is more or a problem for me than for you, I hope that Stefano Baldan had nothing to do with false paintings and if he did, his brother did not know of it. I hope Giorgio did not intentionally put Deborah in this situation."

"Uncle Victor, if that is the case, your friend Giorgio Baldan ought to be more worried about what Aunt Deborah might do."

Count Pesaro de Bonfili genuinely laughed for the first time since he arrived at the law firm.

"I think you are right."

Franco Venier chose that moment to appear, he was ready to leave the office. Count Pesaro De Bonfili congratulated him for hiring his niece. He winked at Rachele and told her he would arrange the introduction she wanted. Franco Venier figured out what they were talking about and simply asked his client if he had time for pre-dinner drinks.

Rachele declined to join them, saying she had several things she wanted to tie down and Gabriele was due to meet her in half an hour.

Professional couples were unusual in the 1920s. Gabriele and Rachele usually talked about plans, bureaucracy, and other practical things over breakfast or on their way to work. Rachele had to solve an existential dilemma. She wanted to talk to Alvise Cantoni. He had seen the typewritten inventory listing only four paintings. She did not. Alvise spent an entire morning looking at that list and could answer some of her questions. Unfortunately, he was also busy with his thesis and spent most of his day at the library. She could hardly ask him to come to the office, yet she was reluctant to meet him somewhere without her husband. She had figured out what she felt comfortable sharing with Gabriele and brought it up over breakfast as she was taking out biscuits from the oven.

"Alvise is occasionally doing some research work for the law firm. Recently I sent him to check a will and the attached inventory. I need to ask him a few questions. He does not have time during the day. Do you mind if we invite him to dinner soon?"

Gabriele had just finished laying the table and was sorting out coffee.

"I have no problem, happy to see him any time. Will you make your pistachio cake?"

Rachele closed the oven door, put the tray on the cooling rack, and turned to her husband.

"Maybe,"

Gabriele noticed her smile and planned to ask again later that evening.

"When do you think of having him for dinner?"

"Well, if you want your pistachio cake, you could ask him. You know our commitments. I'd like to talk to him sooner rather than later but, please, not tonight."

Gabriele stole a biscuit from the tray.

"What about tomorrow night?"

Rachele reprimanded her husband with a look. Gabriele feigned an embarrassed smile. He did not know Kipferl existed until he visited his future in-laws for the first time. He now loved those biscuits. Rachele stood up and started putting them in a tin.

"Tomorrow night will be perfect. Let me finish putting the biscuits away, then I am ready to go."

Rachele had one important question for Alvise, something that had been on her mind for a couple of days. She waited until she served the pistachio cake, the bribe for her husband to sit through a work conversation that could not include him.

"When you looked at the inventory, did you notice any other generic statement that could have meant there were other paintings anywhere in the house?"

She asked Alvise as she was serving him a slice of the pistachio cake, giving him time to think. Alvise tasted the cake, smiled, which prompted Gabriele to ask him whether it was worth the walk from Cannareggio. Alvise just nodded, still enjoying the cake.

"I have spent three hours with that inventory. The deceased must have been very pedantic, not only there was a list of everything, down to the cutlery in the kitchen drawer, but every time something was broken or damaged he put an addendum to the list written in very clear handwriting, adding an asterisk to the inventory. I did not see any generic term that would hide other items in the home. The only thing he did not list were the books. He simply counted those that were in each room."

Rachele stopped cutting the cake.

"I am sure there were more than four pictures hanging on those walls. "

Alvise was too busy eating the cake, therefore he paused for a short time, gesturing Rachele to wait.

"Yes, but they were all detailed. None of them matches the description of the other eight paintings in the list provided by Carlo Simoni. I even asked the opinion of the notary and he agreed with me. The four paintings were listed separately under the heading 'objects of material value.' None of the others were remotely close to the images Carlo Simoni sent us or the descriptions in the handwritten list he photographed for us."

Gabriele could not resist.

"Sorry to interfere, but I am curious. Was the alleged Turner on the list?"

Alvise thought about it for a few minutes.

"I don't think so. I copied the list from the inventory and Rachele has it in her office."

Rachele was lost in her thoughts. Hearing her name brought her back.

"If I remember correctly, it was not. Whoever added items to the original things added the alleged Turner as well."

Chapter Seven

December 1921

Franco Venier and Antonio Penzo, his magistrate friend, were sitting in a café. Rachele's boss shared the broad details of the situation and asked for his friend's opinion. His friend listened, took a sip from the glass of water that came with the coffee, checked his watch, and suggested they should involve the police or the court sooner rather than later.

Franco Venier explained that Avvocato Modiano still had two unanswered questions, so they had asked the court to pause the civil lawsuit against unknown defendants. Once they had conferred with their client, they would pass everything to the police. Then they would decide whether to proceed with the civil lawsuit, naming the defendants, or join the criminal proceedings to ask for damages, even just token ones. Of course, they would provide the evidence they had to the police and Penzo's office so they could start those criminal proceedings.

Antonio Penzo knew that his friend's law firm employed the only female lawyer active in Venice.

"Is Avvocato Modiano your female lawyer?"

Franco Venier knew Venice was the home of gossip. A young female married lawyer practising law in the Venier-Zanin law firm would not have gone unnoticed amongst Venetian legal professionals.

"She is one of my young trainee lawyers. She has already signed up a client and will be the lead in his case."

Antonio Penzo realised his friend would not have tolerated any inappropriate comment. He smiled, looked at his watch, and said he had to go back to the office. The two friends shook hands and left the café. On his way back to the law firm, Franco Venier wondered whether Rachele found it difficult to be taken seriously. He decided to tell her he was taking her seriously every time he had a chance.

Rachele was in Franco Venier's office. They were summarising the case before she called Adalberto Medici to ask him to come to Venice for what she thought was the final meeting before either of them or the police, took any action. Rachele had gone through all her notes and the documents in her folder. Suggesting to Mr Medici to join criminal proceedings as a civil party seeking damages was the best course of action. They would advise him to consider a token amount for damages since he aimed to protect his reputation and if the court awarded him damages, it was a clear sign he had nothing to do with the false certificate of authenticity. Franco Venier listened to Rachele's summary but sensed there was something else in her mind.

"However?"

Rachele thought her boss knew her better than she expected after only a few months on the job.

"I would like to talk to Stefano Baldan. Your friend, the magistrate, should have no problem with that. There is something that does not add up. I would like to figure out whether he is behind the changes in the list of paintings included in the estate."

Her boss picked up her notepad and looked at the diagram. He was not sure he knew what it meant.

"What changes?"

"Alvise saw a typewritten list of the inventory. Stefano Baldan compiled it. Carlo Simoni sent us a photograph of a handwritten list. I hate the idea the criminal proceeding may lead to him becoming a suspect when he may just be a witness."

"How do you propose to do that?"

"Uncle Victor knows Giorgio Baldan, his brother, and he has promised to introduce me to Stefano Baldan. I wonder if we could wait to hand everything to the police after our meeting."

Rachele planned to explain to her uncle that it was important for her to speak to Stefano Baldan before meeting her client. Franco Venier was thinking of his last conversation with Antonio Penzo. The young woman in front of him had a bright legal mind, a strong sense of justice and fairness, and a well-connected set of family and friends. Anybody would underestimate her at their own risk.

"When do you plan to have this meeting?"

"We can ask Mr Medici to come to Venice in a couple of weeks, about ten days before Christmas. I'll hand over all the evidence and notes to the police or to the magistrate, whether it is your friend or somebody else, after our meetings or early January at the latest."

Franco Venier looked back at the diagram.

"What we have discussed so far takes care of one of your two questions. Do you have plans for the other one, the forged certificate of authenticity?"

Rachele simply said.

"I will allow the police to figure that out."

Franco Venier gave her the diagram back.

"How generous of you."

The meeting was over. Rachele picked up all her paperwork, went back to her office and called her uncle to check if he had made any progress in arranging the introduction to Stefano Baldan.

The following Saturday, the Pesaro De Bonfilis were hosting lunch. As the large group was walking from synagogue, Rachele found herself next to Countess Deborah. She knew Rachele would not discuss work on Shabbat, so she chose an indirect approach.

"How do you find the art world, or, better, its underworld?"

Rachele realised she did not have an opportunity for a diversionary strategy.

"It is intriguing. I cannot say I am an expert, but I enjoy looking at paintings and, as you know, I have grown up surrounded by them."

"Yes, I think I have helped your father buy a few pieces. "

"I still find it difficult to come to terms with how much difference a small piece of paper signed by an expert can make to the value of a painting. Take the alleged Turner. I have only seen photographs, but I love it. I understand why my father thought of buying it."

They had reached the top of the last bridge before the alleyway leading to the back entrance of the Pesaro De Bonfili's residence. Deborah stopped, leant on the wall to the side of the bridge, and gestured to Rachele to join her. It was a sunny day, a rare December sunny day. The water in the narrow canal was reflecting the images of the building but also the sunshine. The countess pointed at the water.

"I think I already mentioned that when you look at any art, you need to be careful not to pay too much attention to the reflections in the water. They either blind you or give you a false representation of reality."

Rachele moved her gaze away from the canal and looked at her honorary aunt.

"Next time I look at a painting, I'll remember to wear sunglasses."

The countess laughed

"Maybe metaphorical sunglasses."

The two women started walking again and soon joined the others.

The following Monday, the sun was also shining. Rachele and Gabriele were walking to work enjoying the sunshine despite the cold. When they reached the top of the Rialto bridge, they stopped for Rachele's 'Canaletto moment'. That morning, Gabriele noticed his wife was lost in her own world. Rachele was silent for a couple of minutes, then she turned around, looked at her husband and said,

"Canaletto seldom painted reflection in the water."

Gabriele was not sure what his wife meant.

"That is true. Why are you bringing up now?"

64

"Saturday, on our way to lunch, Aunt Deborah told me that the greatest risk when you deal with the art world is being blinded by the reflections in the water. I wonder if that is happening to me."

Gabriele knew his wife may not be free to share every aspect of her working life with him.

"Do you have an idea of what you are not seeing?"

Rachele stopped one step behind her husband as they were almost at the other end of the Grand Canal

"I am not sure, but I wonder if I am paying too much attention to the differences between the typewritten list and the handwritten one."

Gabriele turned around

"And how would that give you a skewed idea of reality?"

Rachele started walking again, put her arm under her husband's arm

"I wonder if I pay too much attention to the form rather than the content. I will ask Franco Venier if I could share some aspects of my case with Aunt Deborah. Maybe she can help me figure out the right question to ask myself or Stefano Baldan."

Gabriele was not sure he understood what his wife meant. He was sure it did not matter to him. They had arrived at the corner with Calle de L'Aquila Nera, he kissed his wife on the cheek, and they agreed on a time and a place to meet for lunch, Rachele walked into the building where the law firm was, and Gabriele walked towards his office.

Franco Venier agreed Rachele could discuss part of the case with the countess, who had agreed to meet her honorary

niece after lunch. So, once they were ready to go back to work after their lunch break, Rachele took a vaporetto instead of walking with Gabriele. She got off at the Ca D'Oro stop. She thought she knew the way from Strada Nuova and hoped that there were few opportunities to get lost between the vaporetto stop and Strada Nuova. The sun was still shining and Rachele could not help but look at the reflections of the sun on the water of the Grand Canal.

She found her way to the Pesaro De Bonfili residence with no problems. Soon she found herself in the blue room holding a cup of coffee and listening to her honorary aunt vent her frustration with a new client. After a few minutes spent pontificating about how distracting heavily decorated picture frames were, she seemed to realise why her honorary niece was there.

"So, how can I help?"

Rachele took out the notepad with her diagram from her briefcase, which the countess seemed to notice for the first time.

"I am sure that you may find a less masculine briefcase, that one spoils your elegant attire."

Rachele made some vague noises about going shopping with her for a new one, opened her notepad, and started.

"Aunt Deborah, I keep thinking about what you said about reflections in the water. I wonder if there is something that stops me from seeing the obvious. Which is why I am here."

The countess put down her cup of coffee

"Do I have to fetch my notepad?"

"I do not think so. It is straightforward. The starting point is a typewritten inventory of an estate with four paintings marked as objects of value. At this stage, we know that the list did not include the alleged Turner. We then have a handwritten receipt from an art dealer who bought the objects of value, only that receipt has a list of twelve paintings."

"Did the receipt state that all the paintings were coming from the same estate?"

"yes, it did."

"Were the other eight paintings listed anywhere else in the inventory?"

Rachele looked at the list copied by Alvise and the photograph sent by Carlo Simoni.

"Not that I can notice."

The countess thought about it.

"Can you establish when somebody glued the certificates of authenticity to the paintings?"

"No, but we know that the false certificates of authenticity were also attached to authentic paintings. We know that two of the four paintings listed under objects of value, a Monet and a Hoffman, were authentic. I am inclined to think that the other two are authentic as well."

The countess smiled

"I think that the real fraud was in the false certificate of authenticity. They deliberately used them on authentic paintings to give credibility to the false ones. Have you checked whether the same person could have written the handwritten list and the counterfeit Adalberto Medici's signature in the certificates?"

Something clicked in Rachele's mind:

"No, we did not. So far I know that Carlo Simoni, the art dealer from Siena, or whoever wrote his letter, did not sign those certificates. I never thought of comparing the signature with the photograph of the handwritten list."

"Do you want me to have an informal look? I am used to examining artist's signatures."

Rachele already had results, but she thought that accepting her honorary aunt's offer would not hurt.

"That would be great. I have them in the office. Do you mind coming one of these days?"

Deborah Camerini stood up. Rachele knew her enough to recognise determination.

"Are you free for the rest of the afternoon? What about the present?"

The countess asked Rachele to wait ten minutes while she got her coat and 'sorted out her face'.

The countess insisted they walked. Rachele soon found out she had a reason for it. Just before they reached a bridge across Rio Dei Santi Apostoli, they stopped at what looked like an art gallery. The countess was in full lecturing mode. There was a painting in the window that showed an artist's studio and what looked like a painter teaching an apprentice. Deborah Camerini invited her honorary niece to look at that painting before she looked at the card below it. She pointed out how the pupil had observed the master at work, but still could not replicate the brushstroke. She added the same applied to a handwritten page. After looking at a person's signature many times, one can identify those patterns. A painter's signature was the first thing the countess looked when she had to consider whether a painting is authentic or a well-crafted fake.

Rachele nodded. She was busy looking at another painting next to the one the countess pointed out. It looked close to the description of a painting with a counterfeit certificate of authenticity that was not on the list provided by Carlo Simoni. She thought she could remember where the art gallery was. The law firm had no authority to demand cooperation. The police investigating several counterfeit paintings would have that authority.

When they reached the office, Rachele established that the smaller meeting room with an oblique view of the Rialto bridge was free. She excused herself with her aunt, saying she would have to fetch her folders and notepads, and asked the receptionist to escort Countess Pesaro De Bonfili to the meeting room. Once she came back, she found her aunt giving fashion and make-up advice to the receptionist. She waited a minute before coughing to make her presence known. The receptionist apologised, only for the countess to dismiss her apology and tell her niece it was her fault. Rachele hoped she had just thought of smiling, but kept a neutral expression on her face.

Deborah Camerini first looked at the list and at the photographs Carlo Simoni had provided. Then compared the photo of the handwritten list with the letter written by the art dealer from Siena. She told Rachele that she could leave her alone for at least half an hour if she had something to do. It would take her that long to have an informed opinion.

When Rachele returned to the meeting room, the countess was still looking at things. She had a notepad and a pencil and she had written two pages of notes. She was beaming.

"I asked the nice receptionist for pen and paper. Please confirm my opinion with an expert calligrapher before letting the police loose. I have a lot of fun doing these things, but I am not an expert."

She pointed at the chair next to her and invited Rachele to sit down. Carlo Simoni was not responsible for the multiplication of paintings on the list. The way he joined a letter m or a letter n with the following letter did not match the hand who wrote the list of paintings allegedly from the estate. She also checked the handwritten list against the counterfeit certificate of authenticity. They had photographs of twelve certificates of authenticity and the signatures in them were very close. It is difficult to sign anything twice in the same way, even when you have to make a readable signature. Therefore, somebody copied them. Here the countess paused. She was about to deliver important news. She put the photograph of the handwritten list next to the photograph of one of the counterfeit certificates of authenticity and asked Rachele to look at the letter d and the letter l in Adalberto Medici, then compare them to the line in the list that contained the word, Adele. Rachele looked but was not sure what she was looking at. Her honorary aunt pointed out that the writer did not lift the pen between the letter d and the letter l and the preceding letter. However, Adalberto Medici's signature in the form he signed last time he had a meeting at the law firm showed a tiny break between those two letters and the letter preceding them. An expert calligrapher may confirm her gut feeling that the same person wrote the handwritten list, and signed the counterfeit certificates of authenticity. She noticed Rachele was taking notes.

"There is no need to take notes. I'll leave you mine."

Rachele felt reprimanded by her teacher.

Rachele looked at the three photographs the countess had laid out in a row. She could see her point.

"Aunt Deborah, I think you have just provided the metaphorical sunglasses to see through the reflections in the water. I have to ask you to keep the details to yourself for the moment, even with Uncle Victor and Fiamma."

The countess had a smile wider than the one of the Cheshire Cat in Alice in Wonderland. She promised she would. Rachele started collecting the material, but kept the three images, the letter from Carlo Simoni and the one from Adalberto Medici, in a separate folder. Meanwhile, the countess was putting her coat and hat on and was ready to leave. Rachele looked at her watch and wondered if the countess and her husband would join her and Gabriele for pre-dinner drinks somewhere. Gabriele was due to meet her outside the office in an hour. The countess thought it was an excellent idea. It would just give her time for a brief visit to her husband's office. She would ring Rachele if they could not join them.

Rachele saw her aunt out and went to knock at the door of Franco Venier's office.

"I spent an interesting afternoon with Countess Pesaro De Bonfili. She may be just an amateur calligrapher, but she made me realise that I also need to have a long conversation with Carlo Simoni."

She then summarised what her honorary aunt told her. Taking out the three images and pointing out to Franco Venier the similarities between the counterfeit certificate of authenticity and the list of twelve paintings from the estate. Her boss agreed that the written report of an expert calligrapher would be required, but they could proceed with what the countess had established. He then looked at his trainee with the grin of a naughty boy.

"You need to talk to Carlo Simoni. When you do, you might just point out that he may have reasons to join Adalberto Medici either in the civil lawsuit or in the criminal proceedings as a civil partner seeking damages. See if you can sign another client. Talking to Stefano Baldan also becomes a priority."

The telephone call with Carlo Simoni had an interesting outcome. Rachele organised the paperwork to sign him up as a client of the firm. She left blank the name of the lawyer in charge of his account and explained that Mr Simoni's choice was between her and Franco Venier, one of the two partners.

They would both be involved. Mr Simoni also insisted he would come to Venice to meet her and Franco Venier in person. He thought it would be a good idea to come when Adalberto Medici was in town as well. The same day Rachele called Stefano Baldan, he agreed to come to see her a couple of days later.

The time had come. Rachele had spent the first half of the morning writing what she hoped to establish during her conversation with Stefano Baldan. He was now in one of the meeting rooms waiting for her. She used the window in her office as a mirror, looked at herself, whispered 'show time' and joined her visitor. She had met his brother, Giorgio Baldan, twice at the Pesaro De Bonfili, so was not surprised to see an older, but almost identical, version of her uncle's friend. After the usual introductory small talk, she came to the point.

"So far, we have established that there are several paintings, including the four listed in the inventory of the late Alessandro Moro's estate, with a counterfeit certificate of authenticity."

Stefano Baldan sounded surprised.

"The four paintings listed under the heading objects of value did not have a certificate of authenticity. They were authentic. Any edition of the relevant catalogue raisonné[1] will feature image and dimensions of one of the four paintings."

Rachele hoped to finish with as few interruptions as possible, otherwise the introduction would be too long.

"We also have established that. Anyway, although we started this as the lawyer of Mr Adalberto Medici, we have since signed another client who also has a vested interest in establishing the authenticity of every painting he bought from the estate and establish a chain of provenance beyond any doubt."

Rachele noticed Stefano Baldan did not know what she was talking about.

"Who is he? How many painting did he buy when we had the auction?"

Rachele could sense a sensational revelation coming.

"He bought ten of the twelve paintings on the list."

Rachele took out the list, and handed it over to her visitor, who picked it up with a sense of weariness Rachele did not like.

"This is not the original list. My secretary typed it, and it only had four paintings."

They were getting somewhere. Stefano Baldan looked at the handwritten list and explained why the information could not come from the executor of the estate. He could understand the handwritten note. Their list included every object from the estate, down to the bed linen. However, the text showed the auction had not taken place yet. Then he raised his head and looked at Rachele.

"Where did the other eight paintings come from?"

Rachele sensed they were getting close; or, at least, getting closer to the part they would 'allow' the police to find out.

"We were hoping you could tell us."

Stefano Baldan looked at the list.

"The only thing I can tell is that I do not remember an art dealer from Siena buying anything. Somebody must have bought them on his behalf."

Rachele did not expect that. She was now trying to summarise for her sake.

"So, the four painting start out at an auction sale with no certificate of authenticity because they were in the official inventory of authentic works of the relevant painter. They reach Siena with eight other paintings, bought as if they were part of the estate as well, all with a counterfeit certificate of authenticity in the back."

Stefano Baldan thought about it for a short time.

"I think that sums it up correctly. I had to compile a report to send to the four heirs and still have the paperwork from the auction house. It shows who bought the paintings."

Rachele thought they were getting closer.

"Please do it and call me or send a messenger as soon as you know. Our clients are coming to Venice soon."

Stefano Baldan was very prompt. A messenger delivered an envelope the following morning. Rachele opened it, read the content, and was not sure what to do. She called her uncle.

"Uncle Victor, I am sorry to disturb you. I have a quick question. What is the name of the owner of the alleged Turner that Giorgio Baldan recommended to Aunt Deborah?"

"Franco Pavan, why?"

"To cut a long story short, he is the one who bought four authentic paintings from the estate of Alessandro Moro. Could you ask Zia Deborah if she has anything written by him?"

"Can you tell me why?"

"Not at the moment. I hate the idea of unleashing Aunt Deborah's indignation on anybody without clear and unquestionable evidence, and something written by him would help me gain an informed opinion.."

Count Pesaro De Bonfili laughed.

"I agree. I'll ask her. Please remember you saw me at the law firm. Franco Venier asked me to come to discuss a detail of a contract."

It was Rachele's turn to laugh.

"Of course Uncle Victor."

Chapter Eight

January 1922

Adalberto Medici and Carlo Simoni were busy in the weeks leading to Christmas. So they had postponed the meeting in Venice until early January. Rachele's evidence pointed to Franco Pavan as the material initiator of the chain that led to at least twenty counterfeit certificates of authenticity entering the market. Whoever masterminded it knew he had to include some authentic painting to give credibility to the forged certificates. Rachele had arranged to meet Mr Medici and Mr Simoni separately and then have another meeting the following morning with the two of them together and she had agreed with Franco Venier to hand over all her evidence and notes with her theory to Antonio Penzo unless their clients refused to join the criminal case and were determined to have a separate civil case for damages.

The day had come and Rachele was nervous; she woke up early and started baking. She did not think that they now had a live-in housekeeper whose bedroom was next to the kitchen. The most pleasant smell of Kipferl cooking in the oven woke Anita up. She had started on January 2nd and had been with her new employer for about ten days. It was the first time Rachele or Gabriele had woken up before she did. She put her dressing gown on, opened her window for some fresh air, and went to the kitchen.

"Good morning Mrs Mendes, you are up early."

"Anita, first I told you several times to call me Rachele. Mrs Mendes is my mother-in-law, Fiamma! To answer your questions, I always bake when I am nervous. Do you want coffee? I made one for myself a few minutes ago. It should be warm enough."

Anita sat at the kitchen table to drink her coffee, still walking on eggshells. Meanwhile, Rachele stood up to take one batch of Kipferl out of the oven and prepare to put a second batch in. She put the tray on a cooling rack, took a spatula, and used it to take a few Kipferl off the tray and put it on a plate.

"They are still hot. Have one and tell me how they are. This is the batch I prepared before I had my first cup of coffee."

Anita took a sip of coffee and then picked up one biscuit. It was still hot. She took a bite and smiled.

"Mrs… Rachele, they are divine. I only had them when my previous family ordered them from a bakery in Castello[1]. They did not come anywhere close to the taste of this one. You are an amazing baker."

Anita stood up. She had to get washed and dressed. She was delighted she had her own bathroom. By the time she came back, Rachele had removed all the first batch from the tray, taken the second batch out of the oven, and made a fresh pot of coffee for Gabriele and whoever wanted another cup. Anita was still not used to employers who did not expect her to wait on them all the time.

Once they were out, on their way to work, Rachele brought up the subject of children with Gabriele, or better, the subject of Fiamma mentioning children now that they have a live-in housekeeper. In the end, they decided to wait a year and see what happened, then they would start trying. They agreed to be evasive with Fiamma for the whole of 1922 unless they conceived a child. Talking about family pressure, Anita distracted Rachele from the day she was supposed to have. It all came back after Gabriele kissed her on the cheek and continued for his office. She climbed the steps to her office, thinking about what she had to do before her first meeting.

Her first meeting with Carlo Simoni went better than she expected. Not only had he agreed to discuss the next step with Mr Medici the following morning, but he had signed up naming her as his lawyer. Two clients signed up during the first six months of her job as a trainee lawyer. That was great, but it increased her sense of responsibility. She felt she had no room for error, or let her clients, or her boss, down. The meeting with Adalberto Medici went well. She was in her office waiting to summarise both meetings and the planned next steps with her boss, Franco Venier. The receptionist knocked at her door, telling her she had a call from Countess Pesaro de Bonfili, if she was free to take it. Rachele nodded. A couple of minutes later, the phone rang. Countess Deborah came to the point with the speed of lightning.

"Is it true that Franco Pavan orchestrated the entire operation?"

Rachele smiled to herself and congratulated her uncle. He kept that detail to himself for almost three weeks!

"For the moment, the only thing I am prepared to say is that, according to the expert calligrapher, the same person wrote the letter to you and the list of paintings. You were the one who said that the person who wrote the list also wrote Adalberto Medici's name in the fake certificate of authenticity. By the way, the expert calligrapher agrees with you."

Countess Deborah would not calm down. This time, flattery did not take Rachele anywhere.

"Why are you so vague?"

"Because at the moment, that is all we established. There is a possibility that he might have been coerced into doing that, or that he is just the executor and somebody else is the mastermind. However, this is a matter for the police, not for us."

Deborah Camerini was not happy, but agreed to stay away from Franco Pavan until the police had been in touch with him. Her parting shot surprised Rachele.

"Can I hire you as my lawyer?"

"Aunt Deborah, the law firm is already the lawyer of Uncle Victor. Perhaps we are already your lawyer."

"Nonsense. I want you as my personal lawyer. What I do is independent from my husband. I will talk to Franco Venier myself."

Rachele had to end her conversation with her honorary aunt.

"Aunt Deborah, I need to go. I have a meeting with my boss, Franco Venier. Thank you for your confidence."

"You can take ten minutes. He is going to receive an urgent call."

Rachele smiled at the idea of her honorary aunt on a mission. Gabriele would love hearing what she felt she could share with him. She had signed up three clients in less than four months as a trainee lawyer.

The following morning, Rachele was up early baking. This time, Anita got dressed before appearing in the kitchen. There was a limit to familiarity. When she appeared in the kitchen, Rachele was taking out fresh croissant from the oven and the debris of preparing a pistachio cake were all over the table in the centre of the kitchen. When Rachele saw Anita come in, she felt very apologetic.

"Anita, please excuse the mess. I will clear it in no time once I put the cake in the oven. Meanwhile, there is coffee. I think it is still warm. If it is not, please make another pot."

Anita took out cups and saucers, smiled at the sight of the croissants in the cooling rack, and tasted the coffee. It was still warm, so she poured herself a cup and sat down.

"I'll make another pot, anyway. Why are you nervous today as well?"

Rachele closed the oven door, turned around, and started clearing up the mess.

"Well, yesterday went very well. Today I have to ask my clients, can you believe I have clients and I only started working with the law firm last October? Anyway, I am going to suggest to my clients to join the criminal proceeding as civil parties asking for damages. This is not what made me wake up early to bake a cake Gabriele loves."

Anita smiled at the idea that Rachele was thinking of her husband and her day at work

"And what makes you nervous?"

"Late this afternoon, we have a meeting with a magistrate, Antonio Penzo. He is a friend of my boss, Franco Venier, and he thinks I am some sort of bored aristocratic who found an exciting way to spend time."

Anita smiled. She had already realised that her employer had indeed grown up in an aristocratic family, but she was not the typical upper-class young woman who did not know how to spend her day. She was confident that if Rachele had been unsuccessful in her legal profession, she would have opened a bakery, or do something else, anything but stay idle.

"I have known you for less than a month, but even I figured out that it is far from the truth. I am sure everything will be all right. He will change your mind about you. By the way, I almost feel guilty. I enjoy the fruit of your anxiety. That croissant was the best I ever had."

As she said that, Anita stood up to make a fresh pot of coffee. Rachele cleaned her hands, moved towards her and hugged her. Leaving her housekeeper unsure of how to react, but hoping she would end up staying with his family for a long time. She felt Gabriele and Rachele treated her as one of them from the first day she started working for them, a pleasant change for her.

When Gabriele appeared, the table was clear of any sign of the baking session that took place in the kitchen early that morning. Anita reassured Rachele that she did not mind doing the rest of the washing up. Rachele had better get dressed if she wanted to leave for work with her husband. That prompted another hug from Rachele.

Gabriele took a cup and saucer, poured himself a cup of coffee, took one of the small plates at the centre of the table and took a croissant. He then turned to Anita.

"Are we reaping the benefits of my wife's anxiety?"

Anita smiled, moved from the sink to the oven, and turned it off as instructed.

"I think so. I understand you will also love what is in the oven."

Gabriele's face lit up.

"Did she make a pistachio cake?"

Anita nodded. Gabriele grinned and took a bite of the croissant. He was most definitely a happy husband.

81

. . .

On their way to work, Gabriele asked Rachele why she was so nervous. He was sure he had prepared very well. His wife's answer surprised him.

"I am a woman. Most men do not take me seriously. Many men think I will disappear once I am expecting a child. To be taken seriously, I have to be exceptionally good. I learnt it at my expense the first month of University when I was 19. Professionally speaking, I am where I am because I have always been miles better than average."

Gabriele tried to lighten the atmosphere

"I thought you are where you are because you love me and lived in Venice with me."

Unfortunately, it backfired.

"Do not tease me. This is very serious and very important for our future. My professional future depends on Antonio Penzo taking me seriously."

Gabriele tried to recover

"I am sure nothing bad will happen. But, whatever happens, we'll face it together."

They were crossing the Rialto bridge. Once they were on the top, they paused to allow Rachele her 'Canaletto moment'.

"You know, I think Aunt Deborah gave me a very important lesson that I hope I will remember for the rest of my professional life."

This appreciation for Deborah Camerini surprised Gabriele. He did not expect it.

"What would that be? She is not a lawyer."

"I know, but she told me not to be blinded by the reflections in the water. That is why I have got this far in this case. I took nothing at face value. I always tried to understand what came before and after, and whether I was looking at what I thought I was looking."

They had arrived outside Rachele's office. Gabriele kissed Rachele on the cheek and then started walking towards his office. Rachele lingered a bit to watch him walk, shook her head, and started climbing the stairs to her office.

Her clients had the same goal, to make sure their name was not associated with a scheme to introduce false paintings into the market. They both had thought about what she had suggested and came to the same conclusion.

Adalberto Medici and Carlo Simoni wanted to clear their names rather than seeking monetary compensation. They asked Rachele to wait until the end of the month before preparing the paperwork to join the criminal case as civil parties seeking damage. The previous day, they had agreed to take two weeks to think whether to bring a separate civil lawsuit asking for a token damage, but making sure that the court cleared their names. Rachele reassured them that joining criminal proceeding as a civil partner could achieve the same aim and it would be cheaper. In the end, Carlo Simoni looked at Adalberto Medici, then asked what was on his minds.

"What happens if the criminal case decides in favour of Franco Pavan? Will we be able to clear our name?"

Rachele had to admit that there was the possibility that the civil case may not be heard. They both looked at each other and, this time, Mr Medici closed the meeting.

"Then give us two or three weeks to decide. My

understanding is that there is no deadline. We can join criminal proceedings even after the criminal case has started."

Rachele wrote her clients' decisions. Told them she would send each of them a letter summarising what they had discussed and the next steps.

Rachele spent the rest of the morning preparing to hand over the case to Antonio Penzo. She had already organised a photographer to duplicate all the photos and for a typist to copy-type all the paperwork. One of her professors at the law school had taught her to put herself in the shoes of a lawyer defending Franco Pavan. He had written the list where eight fake paintings appeared for the first time and that an expert calligrapher had stated that the same hand had signed the counterfeit certificate of authenticity. That was the only solid and unquestionable evidence they had. The law firm did not have the authority to investigate the financial transaction between Carlo Simoni and the seller of all those paintings, a magistrate might. She was ready for lunch. Her timing was impeccable. She heard Gabriele's voice in the hallway.

On their way home, Gabriele asked her if she had a problem if his baby brother, Roberto, would come to dinner and spend the night. Rachele smiled and said she would not have any problem, but he had to remember to tell Anita. The management of their home was her problem now.

By the time she went back to the office after lunch, her nerves were working overtime. Her outside demeanour was calm and controlled, inside she was very nervous. She hated the idea of fighting somebody's prejudices about women working and hoped the conversation did not go there during the meeting with Antonio Penzo. She had two copies of everything and had divided the evidence in different folders based on what they knew then, and not when they found out about it.

Rachele made herself a cup of coffee and noticed for the first time that the law firm was buying a brand supplied by her family's business. She then stopped by the desk of the finance director to discuss the time she had spent with her clients in the previous three days and discovered that Deborah Camerini, Countess Pesaro De Bonfili, was now her third client. When she went back to her desk, she was not relaxed but was not shaking either.

She had just sat down when Franco Venier appeared.

"Antonio Penzo has just arrived. Are you ready?"

"Ready and prepared."

They joined their visitor, who had a police detective with him. Franco Venier spoke for two minutes, then introduced Rachele as "Avvocato Modiano[2]" with a clear emphasis on the title. Rachele stood up and started summarising the case. She then handed over a folder with all her notes typewritten in chronological order and a typewritten copy of the letters they received. A photographer was due to come to take photographs in a couple of days and then they would hand over the originals.

She then picked the first folder

"This is the first report from the expert calligrapher we contacted. It states that neither Adalberto Medici nor Carlo Simoni could have written the false certificate of authenticity. It includes images the calligrapher used when a handwritten sample was not available."

She passed the folder to Antonio Penzo. The police officer opened it and looked at the content. Rachele picked up the second folder after a pause.

"This is another report from the same expert that states that Carlo Simoni or Stefano Baldan could not have written the list of 12 paintings bought by Carlo Simoni."

Again, she passed the folder to Antonio Penzo. The police officer looked at this one as well.

"This folder has a statement from Stefano Baldan signed and witnessed by me and Avvocato Venier, who states that Franco Pavan bought four painting off the estate of Alessandro Moro. We also have another report from the calligrapher that confirms that Franco Pavan wrote the list photographed by Carlo Simoni and the counterfeit certificate of authenticity based on a letter Franco Pavan sent to Countess Deborah Pesaro De Bonfili asking her to sell a Turner, the one that started our involvement in this story."

The police officer had not spoken yet. Once Rachele had finished, he looked at the final folder, congratulated Rachele for a case presented very well, and for the way she had catalogued the evidence. He then asked her what she had advised her clients and what she thinks of the case.

"My clients decided to wait two weeks before making the choice whether to file a separate civil lawsuit or join the criminal proceeding. It is their decision. I have to respect it, but I do not agree. As far as the case is concerned, I think that the evidence so far only proves that Franco Pavan falsified the certificates of authenticity."

The police officer looked at the three folders in front of him.

"Why is that a problem?"

"Follow me, please. Whoever masterminded this had a clever idea. He glued counterfeit certificates of authenticity to the back of authentic paintings as well and could maintain he did not know the other eight paintings were not authentic. He needed certificates of authenticity, so he wrote a few."

Antonio Penzo looked at Franco Venier. Rachele thought she might have convinced him she was a competent lawyer. He put all the folders in a pile, then asked.

"Why was it smart?"

Rachele was in her element.

"Plausible deniability. He may get away with the charge of knowingly introducing fake paintings in the market, selling them for authentic, and just admit to falsifying the certificates of authenticity to save time and money, believing in good faith that the paintings were authentic. Unless you find more evidence, you cannot prove him wrong with what we gave you."

Antonio Penzo looked at the police officer, who just nodded.

"I think you are right. I have to confess to my friend Franco Venier that I wouldn't mind try to steal you for my office."

Rachele had won her battle.

"I am flattered, but I love my job here and the opportunities I have to grow professionally."

Franco Venier intervened.

"That was the correct answer, Avvocato Modiano."

Later that evening, when she was walking home with her husband, she felt lighter. When Gabriele remarked that the tension seemed to have gone away, she stopped walking, looked at him, and said.

"I won Antonio Penzo over. He does not think I am the bored daughter of an aristocratic family. He may even think I am a competent lawyer."

Gabriele had no doubt his wife was a competent lawyer, an amazing baker, and a wonderful person.

"Did you solve the case?"

"I'm afraid I did not. The police must finish the job."

Chapter Nine

February 1922

In the end, Rachele's two clients decided to join the criminal proceeding. Rachele helped them write statements they could use if their name came up in any articles written about the case. It was a remote possibility because the local and national newspapers had written nothing about the investigation. In Rachele's opinion, everything was waiting for the criminal case. The police officer who came with Antonio Penzo when they handed over their evidence came a couple of times to ask her opinion about people she had already interviewed, but they had not yet proven anything beyond what Rachele had mentioned at the meeting. She knew the police had told Franco Pavan to stay at home and was thinking of interrogating him a second time. They had not arrested him yet because they were hoping he would take them to the person who masterminded the sale of up to 16 fake paintings. The receptionist came to tell Rachele that a woman called Isabella Pavan Rossi was in a meeting room waiting to see her. She had come without an appointment but told the receptionist it was very urgent.

Isabella Pavan Rossi was standing by the window. When she heard the door open, she turned back. Rachele noticed her distress, but she decided to wait to offer sympathy until she found out the reason that prompted her to come without an appointment and ask for her.

"I am Rachele Modiano Mendes. How can I help?"

The visitor sat down, took a sealed envelope marked "to the attention of Avvocato Modiano, urgent" and gave it to her.

"I am Franco Pavan's daughter. My father had an accident last night. When I went into his study to call the police, I found this envelope with a note to bring it to you as soon as possible before I showed it to the police."

Rachele thought she'd better have a witness to this conversation. She hoped that Franco Venier was free, otherwise she was prepared to ask a secretary to come in. She apologised to her visitor and told her it would not take her long. Franco Venier was available. She explained to him what was going on and he agreed to join her and the visitor. They went back to the meeting room and found Isabella at the window, looking at her thoughts. Rachele introduced her boss.

"Please, take it in the best possible way. Your father is being investigated by the police. I thought I needed a witness to this conversation just in case the police wanted to talk to us. What we say in this room stays in this room, but you are not our client. I cannot hide behind client-attorney confidentiality if the police ask me any questions."

Isabella nodded to indicate she understood but said nothing for a while.

"Would it help to keep this confidential if I become your client?"

Rachele and her boss exchanged looks.

"Why would you like to become our client?"

Franco Venier looked at their visitor and looked at Rachele

"I think we can discuss this question after we hear the story. Even if we do not accept her as a client, we could say we are duty bound to keep our conversation confidential unless we think a crime has been committed, or it is about to be committed."

He stood up, opened the door, and asked the receptionist to prepare the forms for new clients, then sat back down.

"Now, this conversation is confidential. We must not forget to make you sign the forms before you leave. Now you can tell us what happened and why you are here."

Isabella took a handkerchief out of her handbag. She clutched it as if it were a life raft.

"In the note my father left under the envelope, it said to bring the sealed envelope here before the police arrived. Last night, as we were waiting for the police, I took the envelope and the note, folded the note, and put everything in my handbag. I do not know what is inside."

Rachele looked at the envelope without touching it.

"Do you have the note as well? Do you mind if we look at it before I open the envelope?"

Isabella opened her handbag and took out a sheet of paper folded in four.

"It was not folded."

Franco Venier took it, opened it, read it, and passed it to Rachele.

"It says to retain us as his lawyer. Can you tell us what happened yesterday?"

Isabella took a deep breath before she started.

"My husband and I are staying with my parents until the builders have finished at our home. My mother is in Rome because my older sister just had her second child. Yesterday in the late afternoon I was working in the kitchen and my husband was in our room changing. He had just come home from work. The kitchen is on the right side of the property, with a window facing the front and a door to the side for deliveries. It must have been about seven o'clock when the gardener ran inside to tell me he had heard a shot."

Isabella was getting more and more agitated. She also seemed to shrink in her chair. Franco Venier was getting protective, telling her to take her time. Rachele was eager to open the envelope but felt she couldn't do it until Isabella had finished. She also noticed the visitor's growing distress.

"Would you like a glass of water? I am sure we could even find something stronger."

"Water will be fine, thank you."

Rachele left the room to ask the receptionist to bring a jug of water and a glass. Meanwhile, Isabella was waiting for her to come back before she continued.

"After the gardener told me he heard shots, I only have a vague recollection of what happened. I must have shouted my husband's name. I remember him and our housekeeper, who is the gardener's wife, being in the kitchen, but I can't tell you when they arrived. I am sure I thought it was strange that my father did not appear. Anyway, we all went out. My husband and I started inspecting the garden towards the old stable and the gardener and the housekeeper were looking near the banks of the Brenta Canal."

The receptionist knocked and then came in carrying a tray with a jug and a few glasses. She put them down near Isabella, who poured herself a glass of water before continuing.

"We were halfway between the house and the old stables when we heard the gardener shout my husband's name. We ran towards the canal banks. My husband saw my father's body first and tried to stop me from looking. He asked the gardener if he had touched it. When the gardener shook his head, he told us not to touch anything. He sent me to call the police."

Franco Venier asked if she was sure she called the police and not the Carabinieri, the army police that was often the sole police force in small towns. Isabella replied the police showed up. Rachele took out her notepad.

"Do you remember the name of the senior police officer?"

Isabella shook her head.

"I can ask my husband and let you know."

"Please do. It may help us if we have to send somebody to check the police report. Please continue."

Isabella took another sip of water

"There is a phone in my father's study and another one in a small sitting room upstairs. The study was closer. When I approached the desk, I noticed a sealed envelope addressed to the attention of Avvocato Modiano and a note telling me how to reach you. I called the police, I picked the letter and the note and went to my bedroom to put them in my handbag, and I walked back to my father. We sent the housekeeper to wait for the police, then I must have fainted. I do not remember the police arriving. I remember my husband, who is a doctor, discuss something with the police. It turned out they were discussing the position of the body and the way my father was holding the gun. I think somebody noticed footprints on the banks of the canal. I knew I had to follow my father's instructions and come here as soon as possible. I had to respect his wishes with no thought to why he wrote the note and what was inside the envelope."

Isabella started crying. Franco Venier was not sure what he was supposed to do. Rachele stood up and went to sit next to Isabella, calming her down. Franco left the room to get the forms for new clients and give the two women some space. When he came back, he was relieved to notice that Isabella had stopped crying. Rachele suggested a quick trip to the toilet to wash her face. Isabella laughed and said she might do that when the meeting was over.

Franco had already written something in the forms. Isabella looked at the form before she started filling it. She noticed the generic reason she wanted to hire a lawyer from the Venier-Zanin law firm. Franco explained it was just to cover the early days of the lawyer-client relationship. They will change it to something more specific once they had gone through the letter and had a clearer idea of what the Pavan family needed, what their advice might be, and who would be the best lawyer to follow them. Isabella took everything on board.

"My father sent this letter to Avvocato Modiano. When I asked to see Avvocato Modiano urgently, I did not expect to see a woman. I would like Avvocato Modiano to be… what does it say here… ah yes… the leading counsel for the Pavan family."

Franco Venier looked at Rachele, hinting she had to comment.

"Thank you very much, but I already represent two clients in the matter of the counterfeit certificate of authenticity. I can only represent you if that does not generate a conflict with their interest. I will confirm after I read the letter and discuss it with Avvocato Venier, who is my boss."

Isabella had calmed down, picked up her handbag and stood up. Rachele could see a person with a steel backbone who just went to pieces when she saw the corpse of her father.

"Thank you for spending so much time with me without an appointment. I understand your position, Avvocato Modiano and I hope you are free to represent us. Our phone number is in the form. Please let us know as soon as possible. Meanwhile, I am ready to take up your offer to use the bathroom to compose my face."

Franco Venier asked the receptionist to show their visitor to the bathroom. He offered his condolences to Isabella and reassured her she would hear from them by the end of the following day. They just needed a day to examine whatever was in the envelope.

Rachele went back to her office, opened Franco Pavan's envelope, and started reading. When she reached halfway to the first page, she stood up, checked with the receptionist that Isabella Pavan Rossi had left, knocked at Franco Venier's office and showed him the note.

"I think we have to stop representing Carlo Simoni. Whatever we decide to do for the Pavan family, this statement may harm Adalberto Medici's interests."

Franco Venier looked at the note.

"You are right. We also have to get a typist to type four copies of the note and the content of that envelope. Have a notary sign they are a faithful copy of the original. We need to give them to whoever is investigating the death of Franco Pavan, one copy to Antonio Penzo, keep one copy for our files and have a fourth copy just in case we need to give it to somebody else."

Rachele sat down, opened her notepad, and wrote her boss' instructions.

"I think my gut feeling was correct. Franco Pavan was only involved in creating the counterfeit certificate of authenticity and writing that list."

Franco Venier looked at her almost with avuncular pride. Rachele proved that a woman had to be excellent to be believable as a lawyer. Difficult for her, but advantageous for the law firm.

"What are your guts telling you about this note?"

Rachele smiled.

"I wonder whether Franco Pavan was blackmailed. I can almost sense the fear in this note."

Franco Venier looked at the note one more time.

"I think you might be right this time as well. Send a letter to Carlo Simoni saying that the law firm will stop representing him. We will not send him a bill and will refund whatever he has paid us. I will check with our bookkeeper tomorrow. You also need to inform Adalberto Medici but do not share with him what we just found out. Then read what is inside the envelope and let me know what you decide."

Rachele was exhausted. She called Gabriele, telling him she was leaving work early. She needed to clear her head to function at her best the following morning. Every time her mind was going back to her unexpected afternoon at the office, she forced herself to think of something else. It never occurred to her she had an exceptional level of autonomy for somebody who had worked in the law firm for less than six months and had passed the Italian bar less than two years earlier. She immersed herself in the atmosphere of Venice in the dark. The city was even more surreal, with areas full of lights and shops alternating with areas that only had one street lamp and the light coming from the homes reflecting on a canal. She found herself in Calle Del Tentor and bought ingredients to bake. When she reached Campo San Giacomo Dall'Orio, she saw Anita coming home carrying a full shopping bag, the result of going with Fiamma to the kosher butcher.

The two women met outside the entrance to the building where they lived and started climbing the stairs together. Rachele could see that Anita was carrying a heavy bag.

"Did we invite half of the Venetian Jewish community and I forgot about it?"

"No, I have Fiamma's meat as well. Her ice-box is full. Tomorrow afternoon she will teach me how to cook the meatloaf that Gabriele likes and make one for herself."

Anita looked at Rachele's shopping bag

"What did you buy?"

"I had a heavy day at work. I need to bake to relax."

Chapter Ten

February–March 1922

R achele felt she had to keep her promise to Isabella Pavan Rossi to respect her father's wishes. She was not looking forward to having that conversation with her honorary aunt, but the time had come.

Her business card said Deborah Camerini, Countess Pesaro De Bonfili, Rachele decided to call her aunt Deborah as she had become accustomed to doing. She entered the meeting room holding the note that Franco Pavan had written to her.

"Good morning, Aunt Deborah. Did the receptionist offer you some refreshments?"

The countess was standing by the window and had not heard her come in. She turned around, almost with a surprised look on her face. She quickly recovered and smiled.

"I believe she has gone to make coffee, thank you. That dress suits you, although it does not highlight your green eyes. It gives you an aura of competent professionalism. I like it. Anyway, can you explain why I am here?"

Rachele took the letter Franco Pavan had written to the countess the afternoon before he died.

"There has been a development in the case started when we found out that the certificate of authenticity of the Turner was not real. Franco Pavan, the owner of the alleged Turner, wrote you a letter. I promised his daughter I would give it to you in private."

She passed the letter to the countess across the table. Deborah Camerini started reading the letter. Halfway through, she took a handkerchief out of her handbag and sorted out her eyes before the tears could spoil her makeup.

"I am flattered and touched. Are you helping him stop the blackmail? He knew that asking me to sell the Turner would expose the traffic of counterfeit certificates of authenticity. He was sure I would have spotted the signature."

Rachele was never happier to see the receptionist come in with a tray of coffee and water. She had just gained some time to figure out how to break the news to her honorary aunt. Countess Deborah took a sip of coffee, drank some water, dried her lips with her handkerchief, and turned to her honorary niece.

"So, are you doing anything to help this poor guy? Do you know what leverage the blackmailer had on him?"

Rachele had already decided what she could share and what to keep confidential.

"His gardener found him dead three days ago. We have already delivered notarised copies of all the letters he put inside an envelope with my name to the police. At the moment, my boss, Franco Venier, Commissario Andretti, and one of the court's senior magistrates, Antonio Penzo, are figuring out how we can help him. For now, I am his daughter's legal representative and she has asked me to carry out the instructions he left for me."

Countess Deborah's face lit up

"So, you have acquired four clients and you have only been working here five months! They must be happy they hired you."

Rachele thought she could share a generic version of another news that would become public anyway once the criminal proceedings started.

"I only have three clients. We had to let go of one because of a conflict of interest with my first client, Adalberto Medici."

"What a shame. Still, three clients in your first six months as a trainee lawyer are quite a result. I guess it comes from the drive a woman must have to be accepted as a legal professional."

Her aunt's last statement surprised Rachele. She was not used to hearing positive comments about her 'stubborn idea of working when she does not need to'. Countess Deborah changed the subject and went back to the reason she was there.

"You haven't told me whether you or the police have found the blackmailer."

"I haven't told you because it is part of a police investigation. We have some indications in the other four pages that were in the letter, but I am not at liberty to share them with you."

The countess was clearly disappointed, but she also understood.

"Can I keep the letter?"

"I still need to keep it until the police tell me I can give it to you. It is the only original we have kept because Isabella Pavan Rossi, my client and Franco Pavan's daughter, insisted that you would receive what her father wrote."

The countess took out the handkerchief again and dabbed her eyes.

"I am touched. I am also flattered by what he wrote. I only met Franco Pavan at an auction three years ago. I must have made a good impression."

Rachele stood up to indicate that she had to go back to work. She showed her aunt out, with no more comment on her appearance, a sign that the content of the letter had shocked Deborah Camerini.

Later that morning, she was looking at a contract when she received a call from Stefano Baldan. He had heard of the death of Franco Pavan and wanted to check if there was anything he could do to help. He had known the deceased for many years. They were in the army together. Rachele told him she would pass the message on to the police. She was about to close the conversation when Stefano Baldan threw a metaphorical hand grenade.

"I wonder if he was blackmailed."

Rachele did not expect that, and feigned ignorance.

"Why do you say that?"

"When I met him, he was in a unit that was falsifying Austrian papers. That was before Caporetto[1]. Later, we both ended up working in the cartography unit."

Rachele was taking notes. This could be important.

"I am sorry but I have to ask again, why do you think he was blackmailed?"

Stefano Baldan was still vague.

"I do not know of any reason. We all have secrets. If somebody found out one of his secrets, maybe he forced him to falsify something for his silence."

Rachele decided she had better err on the side of confidentiality.

"There is a police investigation, but you gave me very interesting information. I'll let the police know."

～

Stefano Baldan's line "We all have secrets" stayed with Rachele till the evening. It was a Friday night and as she was walking to synagogue with Gabriele, she kept thinking whether blackmail was a risk everybody was running. She had been silent between their home in Campo San Giacomo dall'Orio and the Ponte degli Scalzi. Once they had crossed the bridge on the Grand Canal, Gabriele turned to his wife.

"What is troubling you?"

Rachele did not react immediately. He had to repeat his question.

"Why do you think something is troubling me?"

Gabriele had to smile.

"You hardly said a word since we left home."

"Earlier today, I had a telephone conversation at work where somebody told me we all have secrets and we could all be blackmailed for something. I have been thinking of what could a potential blackmailer use against me and, so far, I have not come up with anything. Do you have anything that could interest a blackmailer?"

Gabriele looked at his wife with a puzzled face that quickly turned into a smile.

"If I tell you, will you be bound to confidentiality as my legal counsel?"

Rachele smiled for the first time that evening

"Yes, of course, but you have to tell me first."

Gabriele looked as if he was thinking of something, then his face turned into a smile.

"Nice try, but I do not think I have any hot secrets you do not already know."

Rachele tightened her grip on her husband's arm. It was one of those silly moments that gave her a sense of profound serenity.

The following Monday, Franco Venier and Antonio Penzo invited Rachele to join their meeting. They were friends, and the magistrate did not have a high opinion of women trying to invade a man's world. She tried very hard not to guess why they asked her to join the meeting. She picked up a notepad and a pen and followed her boss's secretary. When she entered the room, Antonio Penzo stood up and shook her hand. A metaphorical question mark was taking shape on Rachele's forehead. Franco Venier could almost see it.

"Sit down, Rachele. I thought we should include you in this meeting because you are Isabella Pavan Rossi's legal counsel. The police have not decided whether Franco Pavan's death was murder or suicide. Antonio is here to discuss whether they should merge the investigation with the case of the fake paintings. We thought it would be worth our while listening to your opinion."

Rachele was sure her boss was the only person behind the 'We'. She sat down and made eye contact with Antonio Penzo.

"According to what we know, Franco Pavan was afraid of his blackmailer when he wrote the letters he included in the envelope addressed to me. It is clear from what he said on the page that explains why he prepared them. He did not name his blackmailer or the person he was supposed to meet. There was nothing in the content of the envelope that read like a suicide note."

Franco Venier smiled. He could see his trainee was behaving as if she were in court addressing the judge.

"If you look at the typewritten copy you have, I think it is on Page 2. He states he was forced to make the forged certificate of authenticity and the inventory that Carlo Simoni showed us. He also explains his plan to ask Countess Pesaro De Bonfili to sell his Turner, knowing she would investigate the certificate of authenticity. "

Franco Venier enjoyed watching the scene. He could see that his friend was forgetting he had a young woman in the meeting and began appreciating the judgment of the young legal professional in front of him.

"I think it is reasonable to infer that Franco Pavan's blackmailer was worried he might reveal his name to the police and kill him. So, I think there is enough evidence to join the two cases."

Antonio Penzo checked his notes.

"Avvocato Modiano, may I ask you why you dropped Carlo Simoni as your client?"

Rachele felt she was in court. She could see Franco's gaze on her.

"My first client, Adalberto Medici, and Carlo Simoni had a common interest in clearing their names. Based on further information, I realised that common representation would not have been in their best interests, so I gave precedence to the client who signed first. Adalberto Medici hired the Venier-Zanin law firm more than a month before Carlo Simoni asked us to represent him."

Franco Venier was very proud of his trainee. He decided to tell Count Pesaro De Bonfili, asking him to pass on the message to Baron Modiano. When he realised Rachele was still talking, he brought his attention back to the meeting.

"…based on a conversation I had with Stefano Baldan, I think you should explore Franco Pavan's military record. My understanding is that before Caporetto, he was part of an army unit that was falsifying documents. I do not know how the army works, but I wonder if you can find out who else was in that unit."

Antonio Penzo was intrigued.

"Why do you say that?"

"Whoever asked, or forced, Franco Pavan to organise counterfeit certificate of authenticity must have known he could create very credible counterfeits. It is reasonable to think that person would have known of his experience in the military."

Antonio Penzo took a note to talk to Stefano Baldan. Franco Venier had been looking at the typewritten notes on Rachele's case. He did not find what he was looking for.

"Do we know what Franco Pavan's occupation was?"

Rachele turned to him

"It never came up in any conversation. I should have asked his daughter, but when she came here, she was so distressed that I did not think of asking."

Antonio Penzo added it didn't come up in his note either. Nobody seems to have asked. Rachele made a note to find out next time she was talking to his daughter. It might be useful. Franco Venier looked at his watch and closed the meeting.

"Antonio, we think the two cases are connected. As you can see, we are willing to share any information with the usual confidentiality provision."

Rachele took that as a hint to leave the room. She excused herself, saying that she had to go back to the amendments to an old agreement originally written in German. Once Franco Venier had seen his guest out, he knocked at Rachele's door.

"You were great. You impressed Antonio Penzo. Don't be offended, he said you have the brain of a man."

Rachele laughed

"I am not offended, but I do not consider it a compliment either. Anyway, I am annoyed I forgot to ask Isabella Pavan Rossi what her father did for a living."

"Given where they live, he may not have needed to work."

Rachele looked up from her notes.

"In that case, managing his assets would have been his work."

Chapter Eleven

April 1922

Anita had been working for Gabriele and Rachele for longer than three months. She knew Rachele was nervous about something when she walked into the kitchen early in the morning and found her employer already awake and busy baking.

"Good morning, isn't it too late to bake something now with Passover[1] starting in less than two weeks?"

Rachele had biscuits in the oven and was cleaning the table where she prepared them.

"Fiamma and the Rabbi's wife have taught you well. I am bringing half of them to work this morning. Gabriele will finish the rest in time, and if not, his baby brother, Roberto, will."

Anita was getting more and more comfortable being treated as an equal by Rachele.

"Can you talk about what's bothering you?"

Rachele thought Anita was getting to know her very well. She liked how they interacted; she hoped Anita would stay when they had children. It might have been only three months, but she had become an essential part of their household. Rachele was sure Anita was running their household.

"Nothing confidential or secretive. I am comparing the Italian translation of a contract with the original German and there is a paragraph that has a major difference. Halfway through making the pistachio cream, I have figured out how to present those differences. I have also made something for our breakfast. They are keeping warm in the lower oven. Can you take them out, please? I made coffee, but maybe it is cold by now."

Anita took out the pastries, tasted the coffee, and started preparing another one. Gabriele chose that time to appear.

"Good morning, ladies. Rachele, whatever you have made smells wonderful. When do I need to take a day off to help clean this place for Pesach[2]?"

Anita and Rachele looked at each other. They had not decided yet. Rachele nodded before replying.

"We have not decided yet. Do you mind if we talk about it at lunch? Anita, will you be here for lunch or do you have another lesson with the Rabbi's wife.?"

Rachele's colleagues appreciated the pistachio biscuits she had baked. Her boss knew she baked when she needed a break from something she had been concentrating on for too long without finding a way out. He took one bite of the biscuits and said that Rachele needed to be distracted from a difficult problem more often. They were in the kitchen with other colleagues laughing when the receptionist came to tell them that Carlo Simoni had just arrived. He was aware he did not have an appointment, but he begged to talk to Avvocato Modiano and Avvocato Venier. Rachele and her boss looked at each other. Rachele said that she had already written some notes regarding the difference between the two versions of the contract. She could give him an hour of her time, but she'd rather have a partner with her. Unfortunately, Franco Venier did not have time, so Giovanni Zanin, the other partner, joined her. Rachele introduced the partner to the visitor and came straight to the point.

"I am sure you appreciate why we have declined to represent you."

Carlo Simoni kept using his handkerchief to dry his forehead.

"I understand why you do not want to represent me, but I hope you may recommend another lawyer here in Venice."

Giovanni Zanin and Rachele looked at each other. Rachele raised her eyebrows, hoping that he would understand she was asking him to speak. He did understand.

"We are not bound to confidentiality and may share whatever you tell us with the police. We may also use it against you if it would be to the advantage of our client."

Carlo Simoni asked if they minded if he took his jacket off.

"I need a criminal lawyer. The police want to talk to me regarding the blackmail and the death of Franco Pavan. I had nothing to do with his death and was blackmailed as well."

Rachele was not surprised, given what Franco Pavan had written to her before he died. He had not accused Carlo Simoni of blackmailing him. She told their very distressed visitor that Franco Pavan knew the art dealer would receive authentic paintings and fake paintings, all with counterfeit certificates of authenticity. Once they knew that, they had to decline to represent Mr Simoni. Rachele had no problem telling the police he was not the person who was supposed to meet Franco Pavan that evening. Carlo Simoni seemed to relax a bit. That was before Rachele continued.

"May I ask you why were you not straightforward with us? It would have been easier and Franco Pavan might still be alive."

Carlo Simoni was almost tearing his handkerchief by now.

"I was hoping we would stop at the counterfeit certificates of authenticity."

Giovanni Zanin intervened

"I am afraid it is up to Avvocato Modiano whether she agrees to represent you."

Rachele was feeling sorry for the man. He was old enough to be her father. However, she could not trust him. She explained she would go with him to the police if her boss agreed, but she could not represent him. She would find it difficult to trust him to be as open with her as it would be necessary for her to provide legal support. But they would recommend another law firm. However, if they asked, they would have to tell them why the Venier-Zanin law firm was not representing him.

"When do you need to go to the police?"

Carlo Simoni stopped tormenting his handkerchief. What Rachele suggested was better than what he had hoped.

"I need to be there tomorrow at 11."

"Come back after lunch. We'll have the name of a law firm for you. If I can't come with you, I'll write a letter to the police based on what Franco Pavan wrote me."

Carlo Simoni thanked them and said he'd be back after lunch. Once Rachele had shown him out, she went back to Giovanni Zanin's office.

"I did not expect that. I shall not represent him but felt sorry for him. That's why I offered to go to the police with him."

"I have no objections, provided you do not have a meeting with an actual client. I am sure Franco agrees with me."

Rachele could not stop thinking of the time she spent at the police headquarters with Carlo Simoni. She was there in an unofficial capacity to corroborate what Franco Pavan had written to her. At some point, the police detective asked her to leave. She was a witness, not Mr Simoni's lawyer. Carlo Simoni's face was showing his distress. Her reassurance that the police had no reason to implicate him in the death of Franco Pavan did not improve his mood. The image of Carlo Simoni looking at her as she was leaving the room was still with her. She broke her rule never to discuss work when she was walking with Gabriele. That morning, they were approaching the bridge from the Riva del Vin. Gabriele realised his wife had not reacted to what he had just said.

"Rachele, are you still thinking of the police interrogation of the man you don't want to represent?"

Rachele shook her head and turned to her husband.

"I am. I can't help feeling sorry for him. He was afraid. I hope the police figure out who was blackmailing him."

"And yet you do not want to represent him."

"I would have if he had been straightforward with us from the beginning. He knew Franco Pavan had written the letter with the list of paintings he photographed and sent us. Had he told us then he was blackmailed, I would have represented him. He wasted our time, he wasted police time, and he was not honest with us. No, I can't trust him and therefore I cannot represent him."

Gabriele had learnt that sometimes Rachele needed to feel him next to her, but appreciated the silence. He did not comment. When they reached the top of Rialto bridge and Rachele was having her usual 'Canaletto moment', Gabriele realised she had continued the conversation in her head. They started walking towards her office. After a few steps, Rachele stopped and looked at her husband.

"We have recommended another lawyer Franco Venier trusts. My understanding is that he is talking to him this morning."

Gabriele got lost in her green eyes, as he did each time his wife was looking at him.

Later, once Rachele had settled at her desk, Franco Venier knocked on the doorpost of her office. She lifted her head from the contract she was reading.

"I am glad you are sitting down. I have a surprise for you. Antonio Penzo has asked me if he could come and talk to you this afternoon. I told him we would call him back after we checked whether you have meetings."

Rachele looked like somebody who had the surprise of her life.

"You mean he wants to talk to me? A woman who thinks like a man?"

"Be nice to the man. I think he had just got used to the idea of women working as secretaries when you appeared in his professional life."

When Rachele entered the meeting room, her boss and Antonio Penzo were laughing. Her boss explained they were talking about the times when they were law students. He told Antonio Penzo to look for him before he left the law firm and then went back to his office. Rachele sat down and opened her notepad.

"What can I do for you?"

Antonio Penzo took out a folder from his briefcase.

"Your confidential investigation of a certificate of authenticity of a painting attributed to Turner started this case, and you read what Franco Pavan wrote to you before his death. I need to pick your brain. My fundamental question remains, who blackmailed him and Carlo Simoni?"

Rachele wished she had taken her folder with her.

"From memory, I think you need to establish who knew that Franco Pavan could forge documents. Stefano Baldan told me they were together in an army unit that was falsifying Austrian documents before Caporetto. Who else was there or who else knew that Franco Pavan was part of that unit?"

Antonio Penzo looked at his notes.

"Who is Stefano Baldan?"

"He was the executor of the will of the late Alessandro Moro. The source of the four authentic paintings included in the handwritten list of twelve forged by Franco Pavan, to imply that all twelve paintings were part of that estate."

Antonio Penzo looked at his notes. He did not find a mention of Stefano Baldan. Rachele had to tell the magistrate how he came into the picture. She had to get her folder to fetch his contact details. When she came back, Antonio Penzo had one more question for her.

"Where would you look for the blackmailer? All we have at the moment are the two people he blackmailed into being his accomplices, but we do not know his identity."

"Do you know what leverage the blackmailer had on them? I asked his daughter Isabella, and she did not know. You can ask Carlo Simoni, but you can also ask Franco Pavan's widow.

I had no reason or authority to talk to her, or at least not until the criminal proceedings have started."

Antonio Penzo looked at his notes.

"I don't know."

Rachele thought about it for a second.

"I have no information on the subject. But I would look at something that happened during the war, maybe during the retreat after the defeat at Caporetto."

Antonio Penzo wrote Rachele's suggestion.

"I think it is a good idea. Thank you."

Rachele thought it was a good place to close the meeting. Her 'masculine brain' had given the magistrate at least two excellent suggestions.

"Is there anything else? I need to go back to my contract, but, provided Avvocato Venier agrees, contact me again in the future. I am happy to cooperate."

Antonio Penzo thanked her for two good ideas for further investigation. Rachele nodded, stood up, and went back to her office.

An hour later, Franco Venier appeared.

"You have a fan, Antonio Penzo said you have a brilliant brain."

He then looked like a naughty boy about to steal the biscuits.

"He also added you would have a more brilliant brain than the average lawyer, even if you were a man. We should consider ourselves lucky to have you here."

Rachele was annoyed but appreciated her boss was just relating what somebody else said. It was now her turn to smile like a naughty girl.

"Well, thank him and, remember, you are lucky to have me."

Chapter Twelve

May 1922

R achele loved Venice in May. The temperature was mild and the oppressive heat and humidity of the summer were still a few weeks away. In May, one enjoyed being outside without worrying about the heat. She and Gabriele had finished lunch at his parents' in Fondamenta del Ghetto and were walking towards her office. During lunch, Fiamma had asked if they were thinking of children, now that Anita had settled in. Anita had spent the morning with Fiamma, learning about preparing meals following the Jewish dietary laws. She was eating with them, like she did at home, and mentioned that she loved the idea of children in the home. Fiamma's unsubtle hints had embarrassed Gabriele, and he was almost apologetic towards his wife.

"I am sorry my mother brought up children."

Rachele was not embarrassed at all

"Why didn't you tell her we have a lot of fun trying?"

"Because she's my mother!"

"And, like my mother, she will keep talking about babies until we have one. By the way, did you notice that Anita also kept throwing hints she would have no problems with children?"

Gabriele was uncomfortable discussing something he considered so private with his mother and his housekeeper. Truth be told, he was uncomfortable discussing it while walking around Venice as well. So, he changed the subject.

"Are you having a busy afternoon?"

Rachele figured out why her husband had changed the subject. She had every faith they would have children.

"Antonio Penzo will update us on the Franco Pavan case. We have two clients who have joined the criminal proceedings as civil parties. We have to be updated to ensure we achieve the best interest for our clients when the case goes to court, but the magistrate does not have to be the one who does it."

"Didn't you say he was a friend of your boss?"

They had crossed the first bridge, a large group was coming out of a restaurant, so Rachele waited until they had walked past them.

"Yes, he is also the one who congratulated me for my masculine brain."

Gabriele adjusted his Panama hat and laughed, then his face settled in a naughty smile.

"You must have loved that. I could have told him there is nothing masculine in you."

Rachele did not react well.

"Don't laugh. You are a man. You do not have to battle for credibility almost daily. At least, I do not have that problem within the law firm, and I should be grateful for that."

Gabriele started a tirade about his wife's skills, almost as if he had not been talking to Rachele all the time. Rachele took it as the declaration of love it was. By the time Gabriele had finished, they had reached her office. He kissed her on the cheek and suggested that if they both finished on time, they might stop in Campo San Polo for pre-dinner drinks with Paolo, Sofia, and their son. Rachele climbed the stairs to her office and Gabriele continued on his way to his office.

Half an hour later, the receptionist came to tell her that Antonio Penzo had arrived and was waiting for her in the meeting room. This time, she took the folders with her notes about the Franco Pavan case and the counterfeit certificates of authenticity. Her boss was also in the room. Once Franco Venier left, Antonio Penzo came straight to the point.

"Your gut feeling that we should look into somebody who met Franco Pavan in the army was correct. Stefano Baldan has been very helpful with a list of people who came and went from Mario's office. Unfortunately, Carlo Simoni still maintains the blackmailer contacted him anonymously. So we are still looking for evidence."

Rachele also had news for the magistrate.

"My client, Isabella Pavan Rossi, has spoken to her mother about the blackmail. They wonder whether Franco Pavan's medal is real. He could have written the citation and the certificate himself. Can't you look in the army records? If the medal was indeed fake, we could reduce your list of ten potential names to those who could have known it was not real."

Antonio Penzo took a note to check the army record. Rachele asked him whether he had any idea why Carlo Simoni was blackmailed. The magistrate looked at his notes.

"I think it is another army story. He did not say much, but something happened during the retreat from Caporetto. Something Carlo Simoni did not want to become known, I am not sure what it is, but we are looking at his army record as well."

Rachele joined her hands, the index fingers touching her lips, her "thinking pose". After a brief pause, she smiled.

"What if it is not in the records? Maybe you could find out who was with Carlo Simoni and Franco Pavan during the retreat. I wonder if Stefano Baldan could help."

Antonio Penzo smiled.

"That is another brilliant idea. I'll tell Franco you are smarter than any trainee lawyer I have met since I became a magistrate."

Rachele thanked him for the compliment. Antonio Penzo said he had a lot to think about. At the moment, they had a list of ten potential suspects and they were investigating their whereabouts on the day Franco Pavan died. He was hoping to shorten that list soon. He would keep Rachele updated.

An hour after the magistrate had left, Franco Venier knocked at the doorpost of her office.

"What did you do to Antonio? Before he left, he came to tell me we should promote you. You are too smart to be just a trainee. He threatened many things if we wait too long to promote you."

Rachele's smile was genuine.

"I am not sure. I asked two questions and made some suggestions where he could look. They have the power to check army records. We do not."

Then she added coyly.

"I was only trying to further the interest of my clients."

Twice a month, Rachele sat down to write a letter to her clients. Sometimes her letters were just a way to stay in touch and to share any progress with them, even when there was no progress. Summarising the state of things was a moment to reflect and think of possible next steps. That afternoon

Rachele realised she kept going back to Stefano Baldan. Had he been as straightforward with them and with the police as he would have liked them to believe? Her aunt's words about reflections in the water came back to her. Did reflections in the water blind them and stop them from looking at the obvious? Were they looking at an image from the wrong angle?

She started drawing a diagram, not her usual one with the circles. She wanted to chart the "operation" the blackmailer had put together. What was the plan? He used blackmail to force Franco Pavan and Carlo Simoni to have a part in it. Therefore, his plan was to sell fake paintings as if they were authentic ones. Where did those paintings come from? Who had access to them in the first place? It was not enough to know Franco Pavan and Carlo Simoni. The blackmailer and probable murderer had to have the opportunity to source the fakes, otherwise, he did not need to blackmail anybody. Or did he?

Rachele was annoyed with herself. She had been thinking of the blackmailer as a man, and yet it could have been a woman. What if Franco Pavan met with two people? Could the blackmailer and the killer be two different individuals?

All those questions needed an answer. She had no role in providing them. Calling Antonio Penzo was the only thing she could do, but not now. She had to make sure that she had a logical theory before making the call. Her assumptions had to make sense, even if there were unanswered questions. She asked Franco Venier's secretary if her boss was free, then she knocked at his door, sat down and started explaining her theory. Her boss listened carefully, impressed by his trainee's capacity to see the core of a problem.

"The key problem to solve is figuring out who could find or paint fakes. You are correct. The blackmailer and the killer may be two different individuals. Antonio Penzo would be interested in hearing your theory."

Rachele thanked him and stood up. As she was walking towards the door, her boss stopped her.

"You could talk to your aunt, Countess Pesaro De Bonfili, about who could source or create fakes at such a scale. She might give you some ideas. You need to be discrete though."

Rachele was aware of the need to be discrete with her aunt Deborah.

"Don't worry, I know very well that most of what she hears ends up being discussed with my mother-in-law. Aunt Deborah may forget to mention the confidential nature of what she was sharing, and Fiamma would feel free to talk about it. Of course, after they have wondered whether I am expecting."

"Are you expecting?"

Rachele was reluctant to talk about it but needed some reassurance.

"Not that I am aware. Since we are talking about it, would it make any difference if I were?"

Franco Venier wanted to sound reassuring. He was not ready to lose his smartest trainee ever.

"Not really. Of course, you would take some time off, but we have no intention of getting rid of you."

Rachele thanked him for being a sounding board, left the office, closed the door, and had a sigh of relief at the idea that the law firm would not get rid of her if she had a child. She loved working there.

Rachele hoped that by organising a chat with her honorary aunt in a café near the law firm, Deborah Camerini would not start talking about children. She should have known better.

The Countess was waiting for Rachele and Gabriele to have a baby, like her parents and Gabriele's parents, but she had class. Instead of a direct hint, she asked how Rachele's sisters, Celeste and Sarah, were. They were at different stages of pregnancy. After the update, she looked at Rachele, smiled, and sipped her tea.

Rachele thought it would be better for her to come to the point as fast as she could.

"Aunt Deborah, I need your help. I need to understand how somebody can source eight fake paintings."

If that question surprised the countess, she did not show it.

"Well, you need to be in touch with a talented painter, somebody who can mimic prominent artists enough to create credible fakes. People who do that copy pictures in museums before creating their own pieces in the style of whomever. By the way, Franco Pavan put a counterfeit certificate of authenticity in the Turner, hoping to get somebody's attention. His widow now has a statement from an acknowledged Turner expert who had established that her painting is a true Turner with a verified provenance."

"I am happy for her and for her daughters. Anyway, you have described a lengthy process to create eight fake paintings. Have you ever heard of somebody collecting fakes?"

This time the countess was surprised, and she showed it.

"Why do you think anyone would do that?"

Rachele was ready with her diagram.

"I do not know, but blackmail was the leverage used to secure help to introduce at least eight fake paintings into the art market as if they were authentic. The blackmailer either had to have thought about it for a long time or had a few paintings ready to be sold. This is the key to solving the riddle. How long does it take to accumulate eight false paintings?"

"I see. You are a very smart woman, not smart enough to only wear colours that suit your complexion, but, overall, a very smart woman."

Rachele's manners prevented her from showing the type of reaction to her aunt's words she would have liked to show.

"Thank you, so?"

"It is a very intriguing proposition. I may have to ask around. The first thing that comes to my mind is a story your father and my husband once mentioned. There was a count who had a house full of copies. He did not collect authentic pieces. He loved art but did not want to spend a lot of money buying originals. Apparently, he used to have his collection valued for fun. He had such excellent fakes he fooled more than one expert."

"Do we know where his collection is now?"

"If I remember correctly, my husband and your father were talking about a story of their youth. So the man might be dead. I only heard of him that one time. You may have to send somebody to search for the copy of his will in Trieste. If he died before the end of the war, his will may even be in German[1]."

"I need the name to retrieve his will."

The Countess dried her mouth with a napkin and took out a mirror to check her appearance.

"You could ask your father or my husband."

When Rachele was back at her desk, she rang her father to see if she could find the name of that Count who collected fakes. Her father remembered but added that nobody he knew had seen the collection. It might just have been a rumour.

Before she acted on her gut feeling, she called Antonio Penzo to share her thoughts. The magistrate was almost annoyed that he did not see what Rachele had figured out. He agreed that the blackmailer and the killer could have been two different persons but, if that was the case, he hoped the blackmailer would lead to the killer. Before closing the call, Rachele shared her gut feeling with him.

"I have been wondering where they could have sourced eight fake paintings. It turned out that Count Federico Maichich had a collection of fakes in his home in Trieste. My father tells me it was a well-known story when he was young. I wonder if it is worth your while to have a look at his will. I can help if it is in German."

Antonio Penzo was ready to try everything just in case it might shorten the list of suspects.

"You think the blackmailer wanted to introduce several fakes in the art market as authentic paintings. To do that, he, or she, had to have the eight fake paintings somewhere. You found the name of a count who collected fakes. Avvocato Modiano, you are a brilliant investigator. Given our previous conversations, I am tempted to follow your gut feeling. I'll let you know what happens."

Rachele noticed he had not praised her 'masculine' brain this time. She went looking for her boss to update him on the results of her two conversations that afternoon.

Rachele looked at a contract for a client of her boss for the rest of the afternoon. When Gabriele arrived to walk home with her, she related her conversation with her boss about children. Gabriele had a delayed reaction to hearing that she would not lose her job if they had a child. They were crossing Campo San Polo when he said,

"You must be relieved hearing that you will keep your job if we have a baby. Many women are not so lucky."

Rachele looked at him and replied,

"Many women do not have Anita at home. That makes everything easier."

Chapter Thirteen

May-June 1922

It turned out that Count Federico Maichich had a villa near Trieste but spent his last years in Asolo, at the foot of the Dolomites, near one of his daughters. So his will was in the state archives at Treviso. Rachele volunteered her brother-in-law, Emanuele, to look at the will and write any details he found of his collection of fake paintings, who inherited what, and the executor of the will. Emanuele travelled to Treviso on a Thursday and gave Rachele his notes the following morning. Friday was always a busy day, Rachele had to finish early, so she put the envelope with Emanuele's notes in a folder and put it in a drawer.

She decided to skip synagogue that Saturday, because she did not feel well. Anita wondered if a baby was a reason for her exhaustion, but Rachele dismissed the thought.

Gabriele wanted to stay home with her, but she insisted he should have lunch with his parents without her. Anita offered to stay behind and make sure she got something to eat. After lunch, Gabriele came back with Fiamma and Countess Deborah who wanted to check on Rachele, but they were hoping to hear the news they had been expecting for over a year. Rachele managed to be social but only drank tea. When the ladies were ready to leave, Anita told them to wait for her. She wanted to go out for a walk now that Gabriele was at home. Once they were outside, the three of them started wondering whether Rachele was expecting. When Anita returned, she found Rachele lying on the sofa and Gabriele reading a book. Rachele lifted her head.

"Anita, did the three of you decide whether I am exhausted because I am expecting a baby?"

Anita tried to look surprised

"I walked with them till Ponte degli Scalzi. We did not even mention your exhaustion."

Anita left the room. Rachele lifted her head from the sofa and looked at Gabriele.

"If you believe that, you believe everything."

The following Monday morning, Rachele woke up full of energy. The two days of rest had allowed her to recover from the tension of the previous weeks. On their way to work, they discussed Gabriele's friend Alvise Cantoni. After his graduation, he had been busy sorting out something for his father and that day he was due to start working at the law-firm. He would work under the supervision of the other partner, Giovanni Zanin. Alvise was supposed to meet his boss at 10am for his induction.

When Rachele got to her desk, she picked up the envelope her brother-in-law had given her the previous Friday. She opened it and read his notes. She stood up and left her office. The receptionist stopped her and told her Count Pesaro De Bonfili was on the phone. He said it was urgent. Rachele went back to her office and picked up the phone, alarmed.

Her uncle reassured her that as far as he knew the family was fine, he had Giorgio Baldan in his office, who asked for his help to convince her to talk to his brother Stefano. Rachele was not happy about it.

"Uncle Victor, I just read something that makes it difficult for me to talk to him, and I think I have to report what I found out to the presiding magistrate or the police. You give me an ethical dilemma."

Count Pesaro de Bonfili was not sure what she was talking about. He asked her to talk to Giorgio Baldan first and passed the phone to him.

"Avvocato Modiano, I am not sure what you found out, but my brother must have figured out that you would not be keen to represent him and asked me to summon the cavalry, so to speak, and ask your uncle to intercede in his favour. He needs your advice. He came to see me last night with his wife and told me he was afraid, but he did nothing illegal except talk too much."

Rachele thought about it. She had listened to Carlo Simoni, she might just listen to Stefano Baldan as well. However, she did not want to be alone with him. In the meantime, Giorgio Baldan had passed the phone back to her honorary uncle.

"Uncle Victor, can you keep Mr Baldan in your office for half an hour? I need to speak to my boss and call you back."

She left to find Franco Venier. He was in the kitchen drinking coffee. Once she finished updating him, he suggested having Stefano Baldan come to the law firm no later than 3 pm. They would see him together. In the meantime, he would call Antonio Penzo and tell him to come to the law firm by 5.30 because by then they would have something important to share with him. By the time he showed up, they might have found somebody to represent Stefano Baldan.

Rachele called back her honorary uncle and related the message. She had just finished her phone call when Alvise knocked at her door. He was early for his induction meeting with Giovanni Zanin. Rachele told him she had to prepare for an important meeting in the afternoon but had always time for a coffee. They were heading towards the kitchen when her boss appeared in the corridor and told her it was all set for Antonio Penzo for 5.30 pm. Franco Venier greeted Alvise, then looked at Rachele, tilting his head towards Alvise.

"What do you think?"

Rachele figured out what he meant.

"I think it would be a good idea if Avvocato Zanin agrees."

"Leave him to me. Alvise, your induction meeting may be a few minutes late. Please be patient. I have an urgent matter to discuss with my partner."

Franco Venier went looking for his partner. Rachele just said to Alvise,

"Be patient, enjoy the lull. You might be very busy this afternoon."

Then she showed him where everything was in the kitchen.

Antonio Penzo was not in a great mood and had agreed to see his friend because he hoped to have pre-dinner drinks with him to let off steam after a frustrating day. He needed evidence to close both cases and take them to trial. He secured a date too early in the investigation and time was running out. Postponing the trial would not have looked good, charging an innocent person with murder and blackmail would have been even worse. The walk from his office had not mellowed his frustration. Even the receptionist noticed he was not in a great mood. She led the way to the meeting room where Rachele, Franco Venier, Alvise Cantoni, and a stenographer had been with Stefano Baldan and his wife for the entire afternoon. The magistrate did not expect to see that many people. He also could not understand why Franco Venier looked so cheerful.

"Good evening, Antonio. Thank you for joining us. We have news you will like, but we need to wait until the secretary has finished typing her notes."

Antonio Penzo looked at his friends with a question mark almost visible on his face. Franco Venier introduced him to Alvise Cantoni, Stefano Baldan, and his wife. The conversation became social. Alvise was teasing Rachele, who had brought a fan from her office because she could not cope with the heat, and it was only the end of May. When the secretary came back with typewritten notes, they waited until Stefano Baldan read them and signed them, and then Franco handed them over to Antonio Penzo.

"Here, Rachele had the correct intuition and Mr Baldan's statements proved it. I also would like to add that there is no conflict with Rachele's client because our new trainee, Avvocato Cantoni, represents Mr. Baldan and he is supervised by my partner Giovanni Zanin."

Antonio Penzo read the typewritten notes and his frustration melted away.

"This is amazing. This is the evidence I need. Mr Baldan, I do not think you are in any trouble, even if you do not wish to be a witness in court."

Mrs Baldan interrupted him.

"Don't worry, he will be in court when you need him."

Stefano Baldan kept saying he did not know what was going on until they paid a condolence visit to Mrs Pavan and he found out who had been blackmailing her husband.

Rachele and Franco Venier were in court representing their clients, who had joined the criminal proceedings as civil parties, seeking only token damages. Adalberto Medici wanted to protect his name and Isabella Pavan Rossi wanted to protect the name of her father.

Rachele was not aware that the last row of seats were all occupied but what Franco Venier had described as "her fan base". Her parents had travelled from Trieste to see her first day in court. Gabriele's parents were there, and they could not leave out Count and Countess Pesaro De Bonfili. Gabriele was there as well, sitting in the front row, right behind his wife. Franco Venier and Antonio Penzo had asked the senior judge not to notice when Alvise Cantoni let all those people in the courtroom just when he was starting the proceedings.

The prosecutor started by thanking the Venier-Zanin law firm for their invaluable assistance in the case. He also welcomed Avvocato Rachele Modiano to her first court case. He explained it was her intuition that led to the successful conclusion of the investigation. At that moment, Antonio Penzo could see six people filled with pride in the last row of seats. He looked at Franco Venier, who nodded and smiled back at him. Rachele was hoping to hide her embarrassment. When the prosecutor had finished, she asked the senior judge for permission to speak and thanked the prosecutor for his kind words and his welcome.

Rachele was so concentrated on the reason she was there that she did not notice that the senior judge had looked at Antonio Penzo before declaring the session adjourned to the following Monday. Antonio Penzo had nodded to Alvise Cantoni, who left his seat next to Gabriele to lead Rachele's fan base out before she noticed them. Countess Pesaro de Bonfili had planned a big dinner that evening to celebrate Rachele's first day in court. Rachele did not yet know her parents would be there.

∾

The team from the Venier-Zanin law firm and Gabriele jumped into a water taxi to celebrate Rachele's first day in court at a café near the office. On their way there, Gabriele wanted to know more about his wife's contribution. He waited until they were in the café. He noticed his wife was not talking and wondered whether she was feeling all right. When they arrived at Rialto, Rachele smiled again. She told Alvise and Gabriele that it was the first time she felt sick on a boat. Maybe it was all the pent-up emotion of being in court for the first time.

Giovanni Zanin has secured a private room in a café in Strada Nuova. They were relatively free to talk. He asked what Gabriele wanted to ask.

"What made you think that the blackmailer and the killer were two different people?"

Rachele was now feeling better.

"Well, I started wondering whether we were approaching the problem in the wrong direction. So, I ended up thinking about how eight fake paintings could enter the market at the same time. Remember, the blackmailer forced Franco Pavan to change the inventory of the Moro estate and Carlo Simoni to buy the whole lot. That gave me an idea of what the blackmailer wanted to achieve, then I realised he had already achieved that. So he had no reason to kill Franco Pavan when he threatened to expose everything."

Gabriele interrupted his wife.

"But wouldn't the blackmailer feel threatened by Franco Pavan exposing the entire game?"

Rachele looked at her husband as if he were a hostile witness.

"Yes, but what if the killer had a different reason to stop Franco Pavan?"

This time, Giovanni Zanin intervened.

"Such as?"

Rachele looked at her glass and felt that champagne had a funny taste. She blamed it on her skipping lunch.

"What if the killer was afraid of something else being exposed?"

Franco Venier saw Rachele's face becoming paler and thought she needed fresh air. Time to end the celebration.

"Rachele's intuition and Stefano Baldan's statement led Antonio Penzo to look at something that might have happened during the retreat from Caporetto and this led the police to have enough evidence to arrest the blackmailer, who gave away the identity of the second person that was with him. Neither of them admits to killing Franco Pavan.."

Rachele did not feel like taking part in a big celebratory meal. Gabriele knew her parents would be there, so she had to be there, so he insisted. Her mood improved once she saw her parents. She spent the best part of the evening avoiding questions about the case by telling them she would answer their questions once the court case was over. Gabriele made sure that nobody asked her whether she was expecting.

The following morning, Rachele felt rested and ready to face the day. The prosecutor has summoned her as a witness. This time she knew that her parents, her in-law, Anita and the Pesaro De Bonfili were in court to see her and she hoped that the novelty would wear off after the second day. It was her turn to be a witness.

"Can you share with the court why you declined to represent Carlo Simoni?"

Rachele was prepared for that question.

"A good part of the reason rests on my opinion. I would like to make it clear before I start."

The judge confirmed he would take that under consideration.

"Carlo Simoni was not straightforward from the beginning. Had he explained to me his actual situation, maybe I would have looked for a way to represent him that would not have clashed with the interest of my original client, Adalberto Medici, who has joined this proceeding as a civil party with a view to protect his name."

"So why was not he straightforward?"

"He did not share with us he knew Franco Pavan had prepared the handwritten list of paintings from the Moro estate. He also forgot to share that he and Mr Pavan were being blackmailed into cooperating in the art fraud we are discussing. However, I think that Mr Simoni and Mr Pavan were victims rather than accomplices. I refused to represent him because I did not feel confident I could trust anything he said."

"Has a client ever lied to you?"

"Mr Pavan and Mr Simoni are my first two clients. Avvocato Venier, my boss, teases me that my idealism and total lack of cynicism reveal my lack of experience."

Rachele's last statement made all the experienced legal professionals smile. She thought the prosecutor was done, and was waiting to hear that she was free to go back to her place, next to her two clients. Unfortunately, that was not the case.

"Still, you accepted to represent Franco Pavan's daughter."

"Isabella Pavan Rossi wanted to protect the memory of her father. I did not see any conflict with Adalberto Medici's case because based on what I read in letters Franco Pavan had left in an envelope addressed to me, I realised he was a victim of blackmail and was a forced participant in the fraud, so there was no conflict."

"Did you share those letters with the police?"

"Yes, I did. We had a secretary type the content and organise several copies. A notary signed each copy, to confirm it was identical to the handwritten original. We gave one copy to the police and one to the magistrate in charge, Judge Antonio Penzo."

"For the court, I can confirm we have those copies as evidence. One last question, can you share how you reached the conclusion that pointed the police toward the blackmailer?"

"Again, I had thoughts, rather than evidence. When Stefano Baldan asked to see me and told me he shared a war story with Danilo Saradei, one of Count Maichich's grandchildren, as he was making the inventory of the estate, I realised how the blackmailer could have found out whom to blackmail and for what. I'd rather not expand on this because it was my idea. I had no evidence. Judge Antonio Penzo and the police found the evidence."

The prosecutor thanked Rachele and told the court he had no further questions. The lawyer representing Danilo Saradei, and his enforcer, Gino Rigoni, did not have any questions. Rachele went back to her seat. The sight of her father mouthing "well done" embarrassed her. She hoped she did not blush.

The next witness was Carlo Rossi, Franco Pavan's son-in-law, who confirmed how he found the body and his conversation with the police about the possibility of suicide. He also confirmed that he did not hear the gunshot but he heard his wife shouting his name and rushed to the kitchen. He remembered telling his wife that her father could not have been far, it was almost dinner time. He looked at the clock and noticed it was seven pm, they usually eat at half past seven in the evening. When it was the turn of the defence, the lawyer insisted on the time, he asked the witness if he had seen his father-in-law in the afternoon. Carlo Rossi said he saw him come out of his study when he arrived home, about an hour earlier. The defence lawyer reminded the court that the gardener had said he heard the shot around 6.30 pm. That meant that the time of death was between 6.30 and 7 pm.

The prosecutor then called Isabella Rossi Pavan. Rachele squeezed her hand before she stood up to go to the witness stand. The first question was easy.

"Why did you seek legal representation and join this trial as a civil party?"

Isabella looked at her husband, and then at Rachele before replying.

"I wanted to protect his name. At the time I did not know why my father was blackmailed, but I wanted to protect his name. He was forced to co-operate with Danilo Saradei, he was not a willing accomplice. "

"You said 'at the time I did not know', do you know now?"

"Yes, Avvocato Modiano told me that it was in one of the letters included in the envelope I gave her"

Rachele felt to intervene, she asked to speak.

"The Venier-Zanin law firm arranged for copies of the content of the letter addressed to me. The court and the police have a copy each with a notary stating they are true copies of the original. I am sure the prosecution and the defence have seen them or have copies."

Isabella turned to the judge

"I do not mind answering, somehow it is not distressing as it was the first time I heard it from Avvocato Modiano. My father, Carlo Simoni, and Stefano Baldan had a very close friend who was wounded at Caporetto and died during the retreat. They nominated him for a medal. Somehow they only gave my father's address. When the army refused to grant the medal, my father decided to forge an honourable mention he and Carlo Simoni took it to the widow. On the way back, my father told Carlo what he had done."

"And you still want to protect his name?"

"Yes, I feel very strongly that the two things are different, my father was blackmailed to be part of a fraud. He forged a citation of merit to bring comfort to a widow. My father might have broken the law the first time, but he did it with good intentions. The fraud is different, he was an unwilling participant. He had found a way to expose the fraud."

Rachele had noticed that Isabella was getting distressed. The prosecutor noticed it as well, he thanked Isabella Rossi Pavan. The judge noticed it as well.

"Do you want a break, maybe a glass of water, before I ask the defence lawyer if he has any questions?"

Isabella thanked the judge but said she was fine to continue. The defence lawyer only had one question

"Did your father look distressed or particularly worried that day?"

"I did not talk to him at all that day. I spent most of the morning talking to the contractor who is doing major work at our home, I mean my husband's and mine, and then I had lunch with my mother-in-law. When I arrived home in the afternoon, the housekeeper told me my father was in the study and he had asked not to be disturbed."

The defence lawyer thanked her. Isabella took a detour to hug her husband and then sat down next to Rachele.

That evening, they were having dinner at the Pesaro De Bonfili again. Her parents would travel back to Trieste the following morning.

Countess Deborah tried to behave and only asked one question.

"Can you share what Stefano Baldan told you that made you draw the conclusions you hinted at this morning in court?"

Rachele was more relaxed than the evening before.

"I think so. Stefano Baldan told me that one of Count Maichich's grandsons was helping him to make the inventory of his grandfather's estate. He told the story behind the falsified citation of merit."

Count Victor dropped the fork and a knife with a clang that made his wife give him a stern look from the other side of the table.

"I can see why they just gave in and did what the blackmailer asked."

Count Deborah saw the good side of Franco Pavan,

"Still, he used a counterfeit certificate of authenticity on a real Turner, hoping that somebody would investigate it and reveal the whole sordid mess."

Her husband looked at her lovingly, then pointed at Rachele.

"Which is exactly what happened."

Chapter Fourteen

September 1922

September had brought rain and an end to the heat and intense humidity of July and August. Rachele had woken up early and gone to the kitchen to make coffee. Anita appeared at the right time.

"Good morning, you are up and you are not baking. I take it as a good sign."

Rachele was taking out a cup and a saucer. She took out a second set without turning around and started pouring coffee.

"I have no reason to be tense. I just woke up, and I did not want to wake up Gabriele, so I came to the kitchen and started reflecting on my eleven months as a lawyer in Venice. Yesterday they promoted me. I am not a trainee any more. Alvise tells me that my promotion came much earlier than usual."

"Congratulations. How will you celebrate?"

"This evening after work, Gabriele and I have invited Paolo, Sofia, Alvise and his fiancée to Caffe Florian for pre-dinner drinks. Myriam will babysit Arrigo, and we shall all go back to Gabriele's parents for dinner. By the way, don't forget you are a guest for dinner. You do not have to get up and help all the time."

Gabriele chose that moment to appear. Anita stood up and started making a fresh pot of coffee. Half an hour later, they left for work.

It was the last day of the trial. Rachele and her boss were in his office discussing the case before going to court.

"Remind me why yesterday the judge agreed with the defence to remove the murder of Franco Pavan from the charges?"

Rachele took out her notebook from the briefcase

"It happened the afternoon you did not join Alvise and I in court. As you know, Danilo Saradei and Gino Rigoni both insisted that Franco Pavan was alive when they left him. The defence found a witness who remembered seeing Danilo Saradei and Gino Rigoni at the railway station at 6.35 pm. As you know, they had already established they heard the gunshot between 6.30 and 7, therefore they could not have killed him."

Franco Venier had found what he was looking for, had put it in his briefcase, and was back at his desk.

"So they are let off the murder charge. What do you think will happen to the blackmail and fraud?"

Rachele put back her notebook in her briefcase.

"When they read Count Maichich's will and Danilo Saradei found out he inherited his painting, he thought he could pay his gambling debt. When his mother told him his late grandfather collected fakes. He decided to try to sell them as authentic works. He was trying to figure out a way to do it

140

when Stefano Baldan's story gave him two perfect people to blackmail."

Franco Venier looked at his watch and realised it was time to go. The conversation continued on their way out of the office.

"What about Gino Rigoni?"

Rachele stopped while they were still inside the office

"Danilo Saradei admitted hiring an enforcer. Gino RIgoni is an accomplice to the blackmail. Do you think the court will also consider him an accomplice to the fraud?"

"Your guess is as good as mine. "

They left the office and walked in silence until they were a bridge away from the court. Then they started talking about the new secretary that had started at the law firm the previous day.

The case against Danilo Saradei, the blackmailer, ended that day. The court recognised Carlo Simoni and Franco Pavan were coerced into helping, therefore they were victims of blackmail, and they were unwilling accomplices in the fraud. Carlo Simoni's sentence was very lenient and suspended. The court granted Adalberto Medici the token damage he requested as evidence of his good name. Stefano Baldan had only been called as a witness and, as Giovanni Zanin expected, Alvise Cantoni did not have to represent his client in court. Rachele's clients had won. They had no reason to be present the following day for the sentence. On the way out of court, Rachele walked next to Isabella Pavan Rossi and her husband.

"How do you feel that the court did not reach a conclusion about your father's death?"

Isabella held tight to her husband's arm.

"I am happy that they did not blame people who did not kill him. I like to think they did not pronounce it suicide out of respect for my mother, my sister, and me."

"So you think he killed himself?"

"Probably, he attached the forged certificate of authenticity to the Turner to expose the fraud without admitting his role in it. When he realised it backfired, he might have felt that the shame to admit he succumbed to blackmail and took part in a fraud was too much for him to bear."

Rachele realised that Isabella Pavan Rossi did not mind the vagueness over the death of her father and was just happy that the court recognised him as a victim of blackmail.

By now, they were out of the building. Franco Venier had invited their clients to a café to celebrate the successful end of their civil case. Rachele steered Isabella and her husband towards the café. Her boss was talking to Adalberto Medici, who had organised an interview with a journalist the following day to discuss his contribution in bringing a major art fraud to light. Rachele admired her client's ability to make it all about him, but she guessed it was the reason he had a thriving career in the art world.

Once they were back in the office, Rachele was surprised to see a note from Antonio Penzo congratulating her for her promotion, the note ended with his apology for not sending her flowers, he would not have sent them to a man who had received a promotion. When she met Gabriele to walk home together, she told him about the note.

"Why do you find the bit about not sending flowers amusing?"

Rachele thought of the words in the magistrate's note.

"Because he made a point to treat me like a professional man, but apologised for not sending me flowers. It is a step up from him praising me for my masculine brain!"

~

The first day of Rosh Hashanah, the Jewish New Year, was also a Saturday. The Mendes and the Pesaro de Bonfili were having lunch at Fiamma's, who had also invited Paolo and Sofia Mondani with their son Arrigo to join them. Arrigo was an honorary grandson (or nephew) for all the Mendeses. At the end of the meal, Countess Deborah stood up like she did every other Saturday and toasted Rachele's promotion. At the end of the meal, Count Pesaro De Bonfili had questions for Rachele. By now, her role in the case was over, so she could answer most questions.

"Rachele, I am curious. I mean no offense. Why did Franco Pavan write to you?"

Rachele moved to sit next to her honorary uncle.

"You mentioned my name. Franco Pavan thought he could trust me when you told me you asked to check on the authenticity of the certification."

"So, it all started when I came to see you at work. And what else did he share with you?"

"Well, there are things I do not feel it is my place to share."

Rachele thought about it for a few minutes, then she told her honorary uncle and everybody else around the table that Franco Pavan knew Aunt Deborah was one of the most reputable art brokers in Venice. She would have investigated the Turner before agreeing to sell it on his behalf. Somebody was blackmailing him and Carlo Simoni. The blackmailer seemed to know something that only a few people knew. Nobody knew Stefano Baldan had shared too much with the wrong person.

Gabriele interrupted their conversation. He wanted to go out for a walk before going back to synagogue and then to dinner at the Pesaro De Bonfilis. He needed some fresh air. Rachele told her uncle to keep his question for another time or go to see her at work the following week, stood up and followed her husband.

They were walking with Paolo, Sofia, and Arrigo up to Rialto Bridge and then they would walk back to synagogue for the evening service. Sofia and Rachele were walking behind their husbands, who had Arrigo between them. Sofia was curious as well.

"I noticed your uncle was asking questions about the case. I have followed it on the paper. One Sunday, you and I will go out for coffee and I will ask my questions, but not now. You need time to relax. You have achieved a lot in one year."

Rachele smiled and looked at her husband talking to Arrigo.

"Yes, but I did not achieve what everybody is awaiting. I did not have a baby, not even expecting one."

Sofia looked at the men ahead of them.

"Arrigo is between his two favourite individuals, his father and his uncle Gabriele. Don't worry, children will come. In the meantime, have fun trying."

After the evening service, on their way to the Pesaro De Bonfili, Deborah had another question for Rachele

"Rachele, I am sorry. I only have one question. How did Carlo Simoni end up with a letter listing 12 paintings as part of the inventory of the Moro estate?"

Rachele turned to her honorary aunt

"Aunt Deborah, do you think it would be rude if I say this is the last question about the case I am prepared to answer today?"

Countess Deborah put her arm around Rachele's shoulders

"I'll make a deal with you. Reply to this one and I will stop anybody from asking any more questions over dinner."

Rachele realised she could not win that battle, but having Deborah Camerini on her side would have ensured a relaxing dinner. So she told her that the inventory for the Moro estate and the one for Count Maichich estate overlapped. One morning, Stefano Baldan arrived at the Maichich estate with letters for several art dealers, including Carlo Simoni. He had already shared the story of what happened during the retreat from Caporetto with Danilo Saradei, but he did not know what the young man was planning. When he offered to post the letters Stefano Baldan thought nothing of it, thanked him and handed over the envelopes to him. Count Deborah was silent for a few minutes, placing the information in her mental jigsaw puzzle, and then her face lit up.

"And that is how the story began. "

Rachele had something else in mind that might need Countess Pesaro de Bonfili's help.

"Now that I have answered your questions, Aunt Deborah, could you do me a favour?"

"Just ask,"

"Please, can we extend the ban to hints about babies and pregnancies?"

Deborah Camerini was very apologetic

"Were we that bad?"

"Worse, you did not even have to say it. Just by looking at

you and Fiamma, I could read the question on your foreheads. "

Deborah Camerini stopped walking and looked at her honorary niece with a serious face.

"I am so sorry, even on behalf of Fiamma. Giorgio arrived after two years of marriage. I was so exasperated by all the hints, questions, and comments that once I burst into tears on Fiamma's mother's shoulders. Leave it with me... but you have to tell me the moment you think you are pregnant."

"You have a deal."

Rachele extended her right hand to her honorary aunt. They shook hands and continued walking.

Afterthoughts

This is not the last book I plan to write featuring the Modiano/Mendes clan or the Pesaro De Bonfili family. As I was writing it, the idea of two series took shape in my mind. So, in the future you will have:

1. Rachele Modiano Mendes, the early years. A collection of novellas that will take Gabriele, Rachele, and, in due course, their children up to 1940.
2. Rachele Modiano Mendes investigates. A collection of novels that will take place between 1947 and… whenever I decide to stop.

Both series will be cosy crime stories. "The Dressmaker's Parcels" almost stands as the bridge between the two. In the future, I will collect the early years in a single large hardback (maybe more than one volume, who knows). If you are so inclined, you can share your views and comments on this and other stories by leaving a comment on the "Books" page of my blog: https://authorsilvano.substack.com/p/books. I do not have a website yet; it is one of my projects for tomorrow. I shall announce when "tomorrow" morphs into "today" in my blog.

Acknowledgments

I'll never get tired of repeating it. Writing may be a solitary endeavour but it takes a village to create a book. Let me start by thanking my beta readers Andrea Rosen, Eyal Ducamp, Patricia Lane, Patricia Wallace, and Tali Schimarsky (?). Their feedback has been invaluable. You owe it to them if you did not fall asleep reading this book!

LWS makes writing less solitary, up to four times a day you are one of several squares in a zoom screen. It's magic, try it if you do not believe it. London Writers' Salon is also a source of friends who provide encouragement and by talking about our book we bounce ideas from each other. The Gold coaches Kathryn, Niamh, Eimar, and Anna support you and help you get unstuck or recover your motivation on bad days. Fellow gold members are a group of cheerleaders who support you and cheer you. Whether the journey is long or short, I would not have been able to do it without them.

This book was not planned. The idea came to me when I was looking at a piece I edited out of "The Dressmaker's Parcels". I would like to thank my friends who listened when I let off steam when I bragged, and when I bored them about Venice in 1921-1922. Thank you Alessandra, Alessandro, David, Eyal, Jonathan, Maria Vittoria, Michelle, Moshe, and Sam.

A particular thank you to John Sloggem who listened when I was stalking about changes in the plot and whose comments and suggestions have ended up in the book, one way or another.

Notes

Chapter 1

1. In Venice, there is only one "Piazza" (Square in Italian), Piazza San Marco. All the other squares are called "Campo", i.e. field.
2. Literally translated, Street of the Black Eagle. The flag of the Austro-Hungarian empire had a black eagle.

Chapter 2

1. In 1921, the road bridge had not been built yet. There was only the railway bridge linking Venice with the mainland.
2. Biblioteca Marciana is Venice historic library based in Piazza San Marco
3. In Italy "Avvocato" (i.e. lawyer) is also the title normally used when formally addressing a lawyer.

Chapter 3

1. Nowadays Fondaco Dei Tedeschi is a luxury shopping mall, in those days it was Venice main post office.

Chapter 7

1. A *catalogue raisonnée* is the inventory of the whole production of a painter. Only authentic work is included in a painter's catalogue raisonnée.

Chapter 8

1. Castello is the part of Venice closer to the Lido.
2. In Italy, lawyers are introduce with the title "Avvocato" (which means lawyer). The introduction was also a way to tell the visitor that Rachele had passed the Italian bar and was a fully qualified and fully licenced lawyer. In 1921 there were only a handful of female lawyers in Italy.

Chapter 10

1. Caporetto was a battle fought in 1917 that prompted a retreat of the Italian Army of many kilometres inside Italian territory.

Chapter 11

1. Jewish dietary laws are stricter during the eight days of Passover and food prepared to be eaten on any other day does not meet the stricter requirement. Also, food cannot be stored during the eight days to be eaten afterwards.
2. Pesach is the Hebrew name for Passover.

Chapter 12

1. Before World War I Trieste and the Istria peninsula were part of the Austrian empire, then they became Italian. After World War II, the Istria peninsula was handed over to Yugoslavia. Now it is 90% in Croatia and 10% in Slovenia.

Villa Kalman's Secrets

A preview of the second book in the series

V enice 1925. Somebody shoots at two teenagers who jumped a fence to retrieve a ball from Villa Kalman's garden. A couple of months later, a young man is found severely beaten and unconscious in the shed of the same villa. Who fired the shot? Who was the young man? Why was he beaten unconscious? Were those events related? Rachele Modiano Mendes is pregnant with her second child. She needs to unravel Villa Kalman's secrets before she starts a leave of absence from work.

Extract from the first chapter

Sunday, 13 September 1925

It was a nice summer day in September. Late August rains ensured that the oppressive heat and humidity of a Venetian summer were gone. Bianca Volpato was watching her grandson and a few friends play volleyball in the back garden. The net was a rope tied to a tree on one side and a pole in the fence on the other. As they were playing, they were talking about what they would do with themselves during the last couple of weeks of school holidays. One boy dived and caught the ball using his fists. Unfortunately, he threw it back very high and it landed on the other side of the fence.

Since the Hotel Excelsior opened in 1908, developers built several upmarket Villas in that part of the Lido of Venice between the Hotel and the lagoon. Villa Kalman was built on the side of a canal. The area was not completely developed and still had a few more humble old houses. Bianca Volpato's husband had refused to sell his land to developers, and the property was now between two liberty-style villas. They knew that the owners of Villa Kalman had left for Vienna.

154

Bianca's grandson decided to climb the fence to retrieve the ball. He had helped the Villa's temporary staff carry or retrieve things from boats moored at the nearby pier and knew how to open the side gate to leave once he had found the ball. A friend, a promising gymnast, helped him climb the fence.

They found the ball, but before they could open the back gate, somebody started shooting from the house. The two teenagers found the button to open the gate and ran out. It was only when they were outside that one of them realised the cartridge must have grazed his leg. The wound was not even bleeding, or at least not yet. Bianca had come out of the kitchen when she heard the shots. She saw her grandson's friend's leg, went back inside, and reappeared with a bag containing disinfectant and bandages. A retired midwife, she dressed the wound. The volleyball match was forgotten. The other boys were trying to find out what had happened. Bianca was listening in the background, wondering who could have shot from the Villa when it was supposed to be empty.

Except the villa was not empty. The owner had asked the manager of the Hotel Excelsior if he knew somebody who could stay in the villa until they would be back in the summer. He had introduced him to Dario Zago, the son of one of the senior members of his team. The first in his extended family to attend university, he was the oldest of six children, and needed a quiet place to study that was better than the hotel boiler room. Dario heard the shots as well and wondered where they were coming from. He took his caretaking duties seriously and started inspecting the Villa from the top floor since he was occupying two rooms that the architect had meant as servant's quarters. He was concentrating on finding signs that somebody had been in the house, so he did not hear the back gate being opened and closed. By the time he had inspected the first floor and the raised ground floor, he noticed the time. He was not in his mother's good books because he had skipped church to study, and could not be late for Sunday lunch. He checked that the main door did not have any sign of forced entry, left from the backdoor planning to check the kitchen, staff rooms and basement when he came back.

About the Author

Silvano Stagni

Silvano Stagni is a multilingual citizen of the world, a father of four, and a cosmopolitan character with a long and varied life. In his youth, he was blessed to have many storytellers, people from different cultures and walks of life. He heard stories from the Imperial Court in Vienna, stories from the Kenyan bush, stories of seafarers, stories of survivors, and stories of fighters. He started writing articles, white papers and opinion pieces during his previous professional life as an expert in the implementation of financial regulations. Now it is his turn to tell stories.

Silvano's blog: https://authorsilvano.substack.com/